MIDNIGHT OIL

Plaything #5

TESS OLIVER

Midnight Oil

Copyright © 2019 by Tess Oliver

All rights reserved.

No part of this book may be reproduced in any form or by any electronic or mechanical means, including information storage and retrieval systems, without written permission from the author, except for the use of brief quotations in a book review.

ISBN: 9781686351211

Imprint: Independently published

One

QUINN

A small plane buzzed so close overhead, I ducked my six foot frame out of instinct. The summer sun was just lifting in the sky but the Brackford Airport, a tiny airfield filled mostly with rich people's flying toys and flight instructor airplanes, was already vibrating with activity. I lumbered across the asphalt as I gulped back the last few sips of coffee. Trey's fire red Ferrari was parked by the building. Zane's Land Rover was next to it. It seemed everyone else had already arrived. I was going to hear it from my big brother for being late.

Chase looked up from the parachute he had just finished packing. "Look who finally showed up. Did you bring coffee for everyone?"

"Don't you rich guys have *people* who do that for you?" I crumpled the empty cup and tossed it across the room into the trash can. It did a nice bank shot off the wall before dropping in. "Still got it, even at the crack of dawn."

"Dawn cracked about an hour ago. Glad you finally dragged your ass out of bed, Sir Wets-his pants-a-lot." Trey quipped as he put his phone back into his pocket.

Zane laughed. "Even after hearing that nickname for the thousandth time, it still earns a chuckle."

"Two accidents in kindergarten," I complained. "I was fucking five years old and both times, Mom was late for work so I didn't have time to go to the bathroom. And my kindergarten teacher, the ferret faced Mrs. Turd Turner was angry from the second we trotted in with our smiles and our Ninja Turtle backpacks until we walked out, broken and sad from a day spent with Turd Turner. And, Trey, don't make me perform my Trey Armstrong meets the mall Santa face to face again." I grabbed my jumpsuit off the hook and sat down on the bench.

Zane shook his head. "That's right, you had Turd Turner. Chase and I were in sweet little Mrs. Jensen's class. She used to knit blankets for nap time."

"Remember those sugar cookies with the smiley faces she used to give us as we walked out if we were her special smarties for the day?" Chase asked.

"Sure do," Zane said. "I was the smartest kid so I walked out with a cookie every damn day."

Trey stared at him with wonder. "How the hell did the rest of us ever become friends with you and that bloated head?"

Zane shrugged. "Must have been my charisma."

Aidan tromped over, looking as big and gruff as a grizzly bear. He was holding a parachute container. "Since you were still getting your beauty sleep, I packed your chutes."

"Gee thanks, big guy." I reached for the pack, but he held it just out of reach.

"Not so fast. I haven't seen the performance." We were all big guys, even Zane, who was shorter but made it up in muscle. But Aidan was a giant. The parachute pack looked like a little kid's backpack in his big hand.

"What performance?" I asked. It was still too early and the coffee hadn't set in.

"Trey Armstrong meets mall Santa. I haven't seen it."

"Fuck, Aidan, yes you have," Trey groaned. "Just let the idiot get his gear on. The pilot just texted that we're taking off in ten minutes."

Aidan ignored my brother and stared down at me with an expression that said no performance, no parachute.

"Actually, I'd like to see it too," Zane said. "I've witnessed it on several occasions, but just like the Sir Wets-his-pants-a-lot nickname, it never gets old."

I put the jumpsuit on the bench and stood up. I pulled the hood of my sweatshirt up and put my hands in my jean pockets, a perfect imitation of an eight-year-old Trey trying to look badass. "Hey, Quinn, I'm going to ask Santa for one of those remote control army tanks." I stepped forward as if I was moving ahead in line. "Nah, I think I'm going to ask him for that Halo game since Mom said she won't buy it for us." I stepped forward again. "On second thought, I want one of those rad scooters that lets you go like a hundred miles an hour down the sidewalk." The entire room was silent. I had everyone's rapt attention, except for Trey's. He had picked up his phone. In his defense, he knew how it ended. I stepped forward again. "Quinn, we're almost at the front of the line. Maybe I'll ask for a new skateboard. The one I have sucks." I stepped forward again. I popped my eyes wide and froze for a good ten seconds before spinning around and screaming, "Mom, Mom!"

Aidan's laugh vibrated the windows on the room. "Ah shit," he said when he caught his breath. "I'd heard about the mall Santa scene, but it's much better to see it in live action." He turned back to my brother, who was still swiping through his phone. "That there, is an Armstrong brother classic."

"Fuck you, Bigfoot." Trey finally lowered his phone. "The

guy had a nose that looked like a red head of cauliflower and his eyes were bloodshot. Not exactly the picture I had of Santa in my head."

Chase picked up his parachute pack. "I had an uncle with bloodshot eyes and a cauliflower nose. He kept bottles of whiskey hidden all over the house. Well, did we come here to skydive or to reminisce about kindergarten and Santa Claus cuz I didn't leave Macy and my warm, cozy bed just to hear about the Armstrong boys peeing pants and crying for Mommy."

I sat back on the bench to pull on my jumpsuit.

Aidan dropped my pack in front of me. "You're welcome," he said curtly.

"Thanks, bro." I pushed off my shoes.

"Sure thing. Hope I did it right. You know how I am about following directions." He smiled smugly at me.

"That's all right," Trey said. "Since he's been working at that medieval joust dinner theater, my brother has learned how to fall without knocking out the little bit of sense he has left."

My brother and I ribbed each other constantly, but in truth, since we were raised by a single mother, Trey, who was three years older, had to be both a brother and a dad to me. I knew that we always had each other's backs, and I could always count on him when I needed support or advice. He was smart, so smart that he and his three best friends from school whipped up a multibillion dollar company out of thin air—and a few trusting investors. I couldn't have been more proud of my big brother.

"Yep, I've taken enough falls from a horse to know that you should never go head first toward the ground." I zipped and buttoned and secured myself into the jumpsuit. Skydiving had been Zane's idea. Actually, it started with his girlfriend Rainsford, who talked us all into our first jump. We got hooked. Raini, who was as wild as she was beautiful, had bored of it quickly. Now it was just a guys' day out kind of thing.

"Actually, I'm surprised you're still working at that place," Chase said. "Usually you've moved on by now. Just like with you and women, once the novelty wears off, you pack up your endless supply of condoms and hit the road."

"I think I'm being unjustly characterized because I didn't bring you a coffee, England," I said.

"The only reason he's sticking it out with the jousting thing is because he's had his eye on one of the food servers." Trey was scrolling through his phone as he blurted it out.

I leaned back with a head shake. "Shit, that's the last time I tell Georgie anything. I told her that in confidence." I shook my head again. "Those darn journalists."

Trey's face popped up. "Ah shit, don't tell her I told you. She's going to be pissed."

I laughed dryly. "Too late for that, bro."

"So who is this elusive woman?" Aidan asked.

I shrugged but my mind went straight to Suzy. "Remember that girl in high school, the one who was older and popular and didn't know you existed but that didn't stop you from ogling her, watching every movement of her sweet little body as she pulled a textbook from her locker and sipped a bottle of soda with her friends in the lunch area? You know the girl. We've all had at least one in our lives."

"Not me," Chase quipped.

I rolled my eyes. "Well, not the England brothers, of course. I'm talking about us regular, mortal guys."

My trip back to high school had left Zane with a glassy look in his eyes. "Hannah Young," he said. "She used to bite her lip every time she walked up to the pencil sharpener. And her ass would sort of sway back and forth like pendulum while she turned the arm of the sharpener. Yep, Hannah was that girl for me."

Trey looked over at him. "Really? I thought you were always wearing a hard on for Rebecca Moore."

"Oh right, her too. I guess I had more than one of those girls." Zane went back to cleaning his goggles.

Aidan pulled his long hair back into a rubber band. "You're not exactly that skinny dork you were in high school. Why the hell are you ogling this girl like a high school crush? Seems like you would have already had her in your bed by now."

I picked up my flight suit. "Suzy isn't like that. Besides, she is living with a guy."

There was a simultaneous 'ahh, that explains everything' comment in the room.

I looked at Chase who had said it the loudest. "Why does that explain everything?"

Chase tilted his head side to side. "She's taken and you can't have her and that is exactly why you want her."

I shook my head. "Nope, you're wrong about that, England."

Trey got the text from the pilot to let us know the plane was ready. We picked up our gear and headed out to the runway. A small plane roared past us and lifted off toward the blue summer sky.

"I think when I get tired of jousting in front of thousands of drunk people shoveling turkey legs into their mouths, I might become a flight instructor," I mused as we headed out to the plane.

"Hey, nimrod," Aidan said, "don't you need to be a pilot first?"

I shrugged. "Yeah, so I guess I'll do the pilot thing, then ease into flight instructor."

"Or you could just come work for your brother, instead of

hopping from career to career," Trey suggested. He had offered me a number of positions inside the Plaything Company, but I was sure it would be a bad idea.

I laughed loud enough that it was easy to hear over the buzzing sound of the plane engine. "Remember, bro, family and business should never mix."

Aidan, whose big strides had carried him ahead of Trey and me, looked back over his shoulder. "Chase's brother, Heath, is working under me in the warehouse, and I've only wanted to draw and quarter him three, maybe four times."

"Yes, but the warehouse is separate from the main building and besides, Heath is older than Chase so Heath can still hold the big brother power thing over him. I'd be going in defenseless."

"Yeah, yeah, never mind," Trey snarked. "Just keep playing medieval knight. You live in a fantasy world anyhow, you might as well work in one. By the way, are you coming to the barbecue tonight? It's your turn to bring the beer."

I shook my head. "No can do. I've got to work tonight. The guy who usually rides as the Red Knight got hurt. I'm filling in for him."

"Did he fall off a horse? Broken ribs from a lame jousting opponent?" Zane asked.

"Nope, I think it was a pickle jar." We reached the plane but my last statement stopped everyone. They turned to look at me.

"Did you say a pickle jar?" Trey asked.

"Yep, the fool was trying to open the damn thing, so he tapped it against the side of the counter and it shattered." I held up my hand. "Four stitches in his right palm."

The guys had a good laugh as we climbed into the plane for an early morning jump.

Two

SUZY

"Babe, can you fix me a sandwich before you go?" Tate crowed from the living room where he had planted himself all day to watch a marathon of Spiderman flicks. The forest of empty beer bottles sprouting up from our splintery coffee table meant he'd be in a crappy mood when I got home from work.

I finished tying the lace on my corset belt, an annoying part of my work costume. "I don't have time. I'm going to be late."

"Please, babe, I haven't eaten and all this beer is making me drunk. I've got to head over to Tony's later for a card game."

I came to the end of our short hall. "You better just stay home. You've been downing those beers like water."

A chip of paint fluttered down from above and landed on my shoulder. I brushed it away. The paint on the doorjamb was peeling and the front room of our crummy rental house had tobacco stained walls. Everything about our living situation, boyfriend included, made me want to close my eyes and wish for an entirely new life.

Tate didn't pull his gaze from the television set. "I'll be fine. Just need to fill my stomach with that sandwich you were about to make me."

"I told you I'm late."

"Well, without the sandwich, I'll be driving you to work buzzed."

"What are you talking about?" I asked and searched around for my keys.

He held them up above his head, still not looking away from the screen. "I need to borrow your car. Mine is out of gas."

"You're not driving after all those beers. Just skip the card game and give me those keys."

He dangled them teasingly in the air. "Come get them from me, you wench. Flash me some tits and I might hand over the keys."

I lunged for them from behind the couch but he grabbed my wrist. It was amazing how the beer slurred his speech, but it never dulled his reflexes. When I first met Tate, he was a tall, fit, muscular guy with a good job in construction. There was always an edge of what I liked to call asshole-ery about him, but for the most part, he treated me right and we had a good time. But a year after he got fired for drinking on the job, a lame ass move considering he was working on steel beams four stories up from the street, he still hadn't found work. It seemed construction foremen frowned upon whiskey filled coffee breaks.

Tate, who somehow managed to be even stronger and stupider when drunk, yanked me hard enough that I fell over the back of the couch and halfway on his lap. His arm curled around my waist and he pulled me against him. A raging erection poked at my ass.

"I think you should skip work and I'll skip the game. You know how this damn costume turns me on." His clumsy fingers grabbed at the string on my corset. I slapped his hand away and struggled to get free of his grasp.

"I'll get fired and I'm the only one making any money." It was a reminder he hated to hear. The beer and his short, hot temper worked in unison as he shoved me off his lap. My hip landed hard on the edge of the coffee table. The impact sent the dozen empty beer bottles falling and rolling like bowling pins. At least two broke into pieces.

"Fuck you," I said through gritted teeth as I pushed myself up off the filthy threadbare rug. Pain shot through my hip and back. I badly wanted to kick his shin but knew that would only push more of his anger buttons, like the comment about money. I rubbed the hip and fought back tears that were brewing from a mix of pain and anguish. What had I gotten myself into with this man? I deserved so much better.

I stuck out my hand. "The keys to my car, please."

He stared up at me with cold blue eyes, eyes that used to make me melt with dizziness but that now only made my stomach twist into a knot. "Told you, I'm going to a poker game." His words were said with slow, sober precision. My barb about being the only one making money had hurt his ego. Not enough, I was certain, to send him out job hunting. "Get your purse and I'll drive you."

A dry laugh shot from my mouth. "I'll take my chances at the grimy bus stop over in front of the shady looking liquor store. I'm not getting in the car with you." I hurried to the stool to get my purse. A bus ride was going to make me extra late.

For a tall drunk, the man moved without a sound. A cold hand took hold of my arm, startling me enough to make me drop my purse. "Don't be mad, Suzy. I don't want you to sit at that bus stop. I'll drive you."

I jerked out of his grasp. "Are you kidding me with the

don't be mad shit? You just threw me into the coffee table. I can already feel the bruise starting on my hip."

"Sorry, it was an accident." Tate put on what he considered his seductive expression, only after a lot of beers it just looked silly. "Look, babe, I'll drive you to work. I'm not drunk." He moved in for a kiss but I jammed my palms against his chest to keep him back.

"No, not in the mood for this, Tate. I need the keys so I can go to work." I held out my palm.

Shunning the kiss had sparked him right out of his apologetic mood and back into angry, drunk Tate. "Well, I need your fucking car because I'm going to a poker game." He swept past me and headed toward the kitchen. He flung open the pantry door, nearly snapping it off its already weak hinges. "Guess, I'll make my own fucking sandwich."

"Tate, you can't drive drunk." I toned down my rage and added a motherly edge. "Why don't you just skip the game tonight?" Then a thought occurred to me. I'd been so wrapped up in the argument about the keys, I hadn't even thought about money. "Wait a minute, what are you using for poker? We've been broke as field mice waiting for my next paycheck. I barely have enough change at the bottom of my purse for a bus ride across town but you've got a wallet fat with enough cash to play poker?"

Tate was avoiding eye contact, pretending to be absorbed in making his sandwich. "I've got enough for a few games."

"From where?" I laughed dryly. "Did you sell a kidney or something?"

He slathered so much mayo on his bread, bits of it were splattering all over the counter. He stayed focused on his task and far away from my questioning gaze.

"Tate, where did you get the money?" The answer to the question was slowly dawning on me. Suddenly, it felt as if someone had just dropped rocks into my gut. "Tate?"

He piled the last bits of ham onto his sandwich.

I walked toward the kitchen. "My grandmother's platinum watch," I said with a waver in my voice. "The one I've been looking for all month." My words grew quiet as I absorbed the reality of the situation. The man, who had on many occasions declared his undying love to me, had taken my watch, the one left to me by a beloved grandmother and my most prized possession, and sold it to a pawn shop so he could buy beer and play poker.

I stared at him in cold silence waiting for him to finish the charade of making a sandwich. He didn't look up from the bread as he laid the knife next to the plate. He finally found the courage to lift his face to me. "I was only planning to hawk it for one day. I needed enough for a few games of poker. I won enough and headed straight back to the shop. I swear I did, babe." He spoke faster as my tears fell. "But when I got back to the pawn shop, someone had already bought the watch."

Tate circled around the kitchen counter and neared me. He reached up with his thumb to wipe away a tear but I swatted his hand down. "Stay the hell away from me. I've got to go to work," I muttered between sniffles. "I'm off at eleven. Don't forget to pick me up." I stormed out and slammed the door behind me.

Three
QUINN

It was that crazy half hour before the dinner and theater show started. The crowd was lined up around the massive building to find their seats for tonight's medieval meal and jousting competition. Not that it was truly a competition since the scenarios were planned out in advance. But the audience didn't know that or at least they chose to believe that anything could happen. The coliseum shaped theater was filled with risers so that the entire audience could see the center of the arena where all the action would take place. The *stage* was as big as a football field which gave us knights plenty of room to run our horses straight toward each other for our well choreographed jousts. Not that it was so well choreographed that we avoided all injuries. Mistakes happened and if timing was off just a tiny bit or if a horse spooked or did one of the many silly things a hyped up horse is capable of, then injuries were inevitable. Even when one of us got hurt, the rest of the actors were trained to make it all seem like it was part of the show. The audience could go right on lifting their pewter tins of ale and gnawing on their roasted turkey legs while we quickly moved an injured actor off the jousting field.

Billy, one of the dressing assistants, finished tying off the last of my shoulder plates. The owners had spent a fortune hiring costume designers to create elaborate and functional costumes for each member of the theater. It took a good hour and two assistants to transform me from plain old, everyday Quinn into the Red Knight. The armor was both for show and safety. It made movement and riding a horse a chore but our modern made armor was much lighter and more efficient than the cumbersome crap the real medieval knights had to wear.

I took one last glance in the full length mirror. Kyla, the stylist, had pulled the top half of my long hair back with a strip of leather, a look that went with the whole knight thing and had the bonus of keeping my hair out of my eyes when I was under the full face helmet.

My armor made me so wide, I had to turn sideways down the narrow hallway leading from the dressing area to the center of the behind the scenes activity. The groomers would have the horses ready and waiting in all their medieval regalia. I was on Archer tonight. He tended to ride hot when there was a big, boisterous crowd. And from the hum of noise outside the building walls, it was going to be one of those nights.

I passed the corridor opening that led to the kitchens and food service area. Suzy, the server I'd been admiring from afar, was lifting a tray of glasses onto her hip. Her pretty face scrunched as she winced in pain. She quickly shifted the tray to the other hip. I dashed down the hall to help her. I was, after all, a knight.

"Fair lady, doth thou need help with thy tray?" I asked in my deep knight's voice.

She shook her head and that smile of hers, the one that

could light a thousand candles, brightened her face. "If it isn't my favorite knight to the rescue," she said lightly

I took the tray of glasses from her. "Where to, milady?"

"The red section. I'm one of your serving wenches tonight." Her pale blue eyes always knocked me momentarily senseless.

"If only that were true in every sense, milady. For you have already captured every inch of my soul with those powder blue eyes and that heart melting smile."

She rolled her eyes. "Shouldn't you be saving that mush for the fair Princess Gwendolyn? I've heard that she was your latest conquest, both on and off the jousting field."

I feigned outrage and followed her to the corridor that led to the dining arena. "Those scandalous rumors are—well, mostly true." I popped out of my knightly character. "Gwen and I had a thing for about a month, but it's over. I've definitely learned my lesson about dating women I work with." My big boots thundered in the corridor. We reached the dining area door. Suzy held it open for me as I shambled past in my unwieldy costume with the tray of glasses.

She had just enough dimple in her right cheek to make a man crazy. "I'm proud of you, Quinn. It only took you—what —fifteen women to finally learn your lesson? Or maybe you just ran out of prospects."

I followed her to her station in the red section and put the tray down. "I haven't run out of prospects," I said with all seriousness as I gazed down at her. I had been crushing on Suzy Riley since I started working at the Medieval Joust Theater but she was in a relationship. And I'd already convinced myself she was way too good for me. Just like she was way too good for the job and the asshole she was dating. I'd only met him twice, once at a holiday party and once at a company picnic. I'd instantly sized him up as a complete fucking jerk who had no business with a girl like Suzy. Of course, that could have just been the jealousy talking but still, it would have been satisfying as fuck to throw my fist in the guy's face just once.

There was an edge of sadness in her laugh. "Trust me the last thing I need in my already screwed up life is Quinn Armstrong, otherwise known in this building and I'm sure everywhere past these walls, as the tall, dark player."

I took lightly hold of her hand. "Not true. Just waiting for the right wench to own my heart. Actually, she already does, but she doesn't seem to want to own it. Just remember, Suzy Q, when you're tired of being a serving wench, this knight is waiting to make you his fair maiden."

She laughed. "Go get on your horse, crazy man, before I start to believe your bullshit."

I lifted her hand to my mouth and kissed it before peering one last time into those unbelievable blue eyes. "It's not bullshit. One day you'll come to your senses and leave that guy—" I straightened. She looked so small and frail and more than a little lost as she gazed up at me. "I'll be waiting for you, Suzy Q."

Her cheeks turned pink and she held back a smile. "Thanks for the help with the trays. By the way, does the Red Knight win tonight?" she called to me.

I looked back. "Nope, I take a dive after the first joust. So you better keep those pints filled." The audience members tended to get pretty damn competitive during the show, and when their knight was defeated, things could get rowdy. "I bid you ado, my fair lady and remember what I said." I reached the door.

"I thought you were done dating women at work," she called back to me.

I looked over my shoulder at her. The corset belt was cinched tightly around her tiny waist, accentuating the curves above and below it. I had seen her without her costume and her body was just as delicious without the saucy wench costume and corset. I'd spent plenty of time thinking about holding those curves and running my mouth along her creamy skin.

"For you, Suzy Q, I would break all the rules." I winked at her and walked out the door.

Four

SUZY

I hadn't realized how badly I'd bruised myself on the coffee table until I started hoisting heavy trays and leaning over tables. Two aspirins had gotten me through a long, loud dinner shift. I was thrilled when the work night ended. I only wished I was heading home to something altogether more pleasant and enjoyable than my depressing little rental and my even more depressing boyfriend.

I'd pushed the heartbreak of losing my grandmother's watch to a game of poker out of my mind once I got to work. The job was so hectic, I needed to be on my toes and ready for anything. At least tonight there weren't any crude, rude drunks, like my boyfriend, to fend off. Occasionally, a dinner guest or party got too fired up and the big mugs of beer didn't help. The management frowned on us complaining about harassment. They rarely asked a guest to leave. They didn't like the negative publicity. Instead, we servers were supposed just grin and stay polite and avoid grabby hands and inappropriate advances. Easier said than done in a crowded dining hall.

I sent another text to Tate. "I'm waiting on the east side

of the building, near the parking lot. Hurry up, I'm cold and tired." It was my second text to remind him that he had to pick me up since he had so boldly helped himself to my car. I dropped the phone into my purse and sat on the bench outside the building.

For a summer night, it was a touch chilly, but I had left the house in such a state of stress I'd forgotten my sweater. I crossed my arms around myself for warmth. Most everyone else had already left for the night, but there were a few cars in the lot, including Quinn's silver Porsche. His car was easy to spot because he was the only employee who drove a car that was worth three full years of pay. The Red Knight's horse had stumbled during the joust and knowing Quinn, he had stuck around to make sure the animal was all right. I didn't know too much about his personal life except what I'd heard through snippets of conversation with my coworkers. Apparently, Quinn's older brother was co-owner of a multi-billion dollar company that sold, of all things, monthly subscriptions for adult toys.

Quinn Armstrong was one of those men who could draw all the energy in the room right toward him. It helped that he was extraordinarily handsome, built like a superhero and yet still managed to be charming. Normally, men with all the physical attributes lacked in personality but Quinn was different. It was one of the reasons every unattached woman at the dinner theater had at one point or another dated the man. I would be lying if I didn't admit to finding myself in the occasional erotic daydream with Quinn. The man oozed sexual magnetism. Just like this evening when he helped me with the tray, he was constantly teasing me, flirting with me, telling me he was waiting for me to give up on Tate. While it seemed I was slowly, truly giving up on Tate, I was convinced the last thing I needed was one of Quinn's short, fiery flings. And from what I'd heard, again through the gossip tree, they were indeed *fiery*. It seemed along with the good looks and charming personality, Quinn, according to coworkers with firsthand knowledge, definitely knew his way around a woman's body.

Tate and I had a sex life that was occasionally good but usually mediocre. That was mostly due to his selfish style in bed, where his climax was paramount and mine was just a nice side benefit. For that past year, I had shunned his advances more than warmed up to them. I told myself it was because I was tired from work, but deep down, I knew it was because my feelings for Tate were fading into a dull gray emptiness.

I checked my phone but there was no message from Tate. I swiped my thumb over the phone icon. It rang once and went straight to voicemail. He had either turned it off or forgotten to charge it. "What an ass." I dropped the phone into my purse and stared out at the road. During the day, it was a busy four lane street, but at this hour, it was deserted . . . and dark. It was a one mile walk to the nearest bus stop and my feet were tired. Not to mention that the bruise on my hip was so tender every step hurt.

The back door opened and Quinn stepped out. He was busy texting and didn't notice me sitting on the bench. I kept quiet and watched his tall, broad shouldered figure cross the parking lot to his car. He walked with that easy, confident swagger that fit his personality perfectly. I rested my head back against the brick wall behind me and closed my eyes. I briefly allowed myself a few hot moments of imagining myself in his capable arms. Quinn's large hands sweeping over my naked skin, his tongue teasing my taught nipple before making its way to my aching pussy. Tingling heat unfurled between my legs. Just fantasizing about the man, while sitting on a cold hard bench and leaning against a rough brick wall, produced more physical reaction than five minutes of Tate's idea of rushed, clumsy foreplay. A flicker of envy went through me as I thought about my coworkers getting to experience a good, attentive long fuck with Quinn Armstrong. Maybe it would be worth the heartbreak of knowing that he would soon move on to his next conquest just to experience a few luscious nights in Quinn's bed.

Headlights flashed across my face rousing me from my thoughts. I opened my eyes and squinted into the strong beam of light. The Porsche turned off and Quinn climbed out of the car. He had taken the leather strap from his hair, and it hung long and loose over his shoulders. He had pulled on a black sports coat over a green shirt. "Suzy Q, what on earth are you doing out here all alone in the shadows?"

Quinn had started calling me Suzy Q from the first day we met. Brenda, the casting director, had been so thrilled at landing her new Red Knight, she had personally walked him around to introduce him to the rest of us. He broke right into an impressive version of Creedence Clearwater's *Suzy Q* when Brenda told him my name. It wasn't the first time someone had called me Suzy Q but it was certainly the most memorable.

I crossed my arms tighter against the cold. "I'm just waiting for Tate to pick me up. He needed my car tonight."

Quinn removed his coat. "Stand up so I can drop this around your shoulders. I don't need it tonight anyhow. I was supposed to head to a party, but I decided to skip it and head home."

"Are you sure? I'll probably only be here a few more minutes."

He held the coat up. "Come on. You can't be sitting out here in that wench costume. You're likely to attract all kinds of vagabonds and pillagers."

I stood to be wrapped in the coat. "I definitely don't want

to attract pillagers, but I've heard vagabonds are quite gentlemanly in the sack."

His deep, low laugh caused his warm breath to tickle my forehead as he reached behind me with the coat. I stared straight at his masculine throat and took the opportunity to breathe in the scent of his aftershave, a mellow, pleasant scent, an expensive one, no doubt. Men in Porsches didn't splash on the drug store bargain stuff.

I realized then, with a certain amount of shock, that we had never stood quite so close. His unintentional nearness sent a shiver through me.

"See, you were cold. Good thing I had my coat." Quinn mistook the slight tremble as a result of the cold, but I knew it came from an entirely different source. There was no denying it, when he was close enough to see every long spike of eyelash and every bit of stubble from his five-o'clock shadow, Quinn Armstrong was a fucking male masterpiece.

He pulled the oversized coat around my shoulders and pinched it shut as he tilted his head to look at my face. "Better?"

I went from sitting on a frigid bench in my thin cotton peasant blouse to being draped and swaddled in Quinn's warm masculine scent. I was long past *better*.

"How do you manage it?" I asked as I took over gripping the coat shut around me. The broad shoulders were like planks jutting out from my neck. I could have wrapped myself in the coat twice but I felt cozy.

"Manage what?" He motioned to the bench and sat next to me. "I'm going to wait with you until what's his name shows up."

"How do you manage to make a girl feel like swooning just by wrapping her in your coat?"

He looked over with that impish grin he wore when he

was feeling extra cocky. "Are you close to swooning, Suzy Q? Then my night has been a triumph after all."

I laughed lightly. The sound of it spread out and disappeared into the dark night. All of the despair I'd been feeling about my life seemed to float off with it. My bench partner's coat was more magical than I first thought. Just feeling warm, protected and suddenly the center of someone's concern had done it. I lacked all those things with Tate.

"You know, Quinn, it's a shame you're such a player, bouncing from one girl to the next. You would make some unbelievably lucky woman an incredible boyfriend."

"Ouch. Don't believe all the rumors. And thank you. There I think I addressed everything you just tossed at me. I'm not that much of a player—"

I cleared my throat. "I've been inside the dressing room when the actresses are getting ready. Let me just say, I know more personal details about you, then you probably know yourself."

"Shit." His face dropped. He pushed his long hair behind his ear, giving me a stunning view of his perfectly chiseled profile. There was just enough bump on his nose to be extra masculine, which worked perfectly with his strong jaw. "Sometimes I wish we didn't work together. That way I could be a complete stranger, and you wouldn't already have such a bad opinion of me."

Without thinking, I reached over and put my hand on top of his. His large, capable hand was warm. For a fleeting second, my mind dashed back to the short fantasy I was having just seconds before. Some of the heat was still nestled between my legs. Or that might just have been from sitting next to him.

"I don't think badly of you, Quinn. Frankly, you're one of the most decent guys in the group. You like women and you like fooling around. I can't fault you for that, or I'd have to fault half the men in the world. You just happen to be extremely successful at it."

"Huh, not sure if that makes me feel any better, but I promise you, it would be different with you, Suzy Q."

The oversized coat shifted around me as I laughed. "I hate to sound cliché, but I bet you say that to all the girls."

"Not true." He turned slightly to look at me. I realized I had left my hand on his and reluctantly pulled it away. "With the exception of Britney Hooper in sixth grade, I have never said that to any woman. And I meant every word of it."

I drew the coat tighter around me and hid my smile beneath the tall collar. "Britney Hooper, eh?"

He leaned back against the brick wall and stared out at the darkness. "Yeah, she had the cutest spray of freckles and long hair that she clipped back with little rhinestone butterflies. She broke my heart. She used to ride over to our house on her bicycle to play video games. I thought she was there to see me. Turns out she had a big crush on my older brother." He shook his head without lifting it from the wall. "I felt so cheap and used."

I chuckled. "That must have stung. I was going to say that I felt honored to be in the same lofty group as Britney Hooper, but it sounds like she fell from grace after that."

Quinn sat up straight, reminding me just how tall he was. "She did indeed and it was all for naught. Trey was three years older, and there was never any shortage of girls in his teenage world."

"I've heard he's quite the businessman. Probably no shortage of women now either," I suggested.

"There was plenty for awhile but now there is just the one. Georgie, his soulmate. She's an award winning journalist. I think he might even pop the question soon. So, you see, we Armstrongs can commit. It just takes finding the right person. And speaking of the *wrong* person, it seems like your ride is not coming. I'd be happy to give you a ride home."

I was more than embarrassed that Tate had decided to just leave me sitting alone outside of work. Quinn wasn't showing pity but I was sure it was there beneath the layers of hunkiness.

I pulled out my phone, knowing full well that Tate hadn't texted or called, but I wanted to at least give the illusion that he might have been trying to contact me to let me know he'd be late. To save face, I made up a lie and pretended there had been a text. "Actually, he says he's on his way. You go ahead, Quinn. And thanks for keeping me company." I stood up to take off the coat.

He pushed to his feet and pulled the coat shut around me again, giving me a little tug so that I inadvertently fell against his hard chest. He didn't release me. I stayed pressed against him. Every inch of him exuded warmth, strength, confidence. I wondered how dizzying it would feel to be wrapped in his strong arms. With slow reluctance, he released me and my body peeled away from his. Heat seemed to swirl around us as we both gazed into each other's eyes for a silent few seconds.

"You can keep the coat for now. Seeing you wrapped up in it is the best thing I've seen in a long time."

I shrugged my thin shoulders beneath the giant coat. "Maybe I'll start a new fashion trend. Thanks again." I motioned toward his car. "You should get going. I'm sure you're tired after your performance. And Tate will be here any minute so I'm fine."

He pointed at me. "Ah ha, so you were lying about Tate coming to pick you up."

I blinked up at him in question. "No, really. He's coming," I said with little conviction. My cheeks heated with shame. I sighed. "How did you know?"

"The coat. Most women wouldn't stay wrapped in another

guy's coat while they were waiting for their boyfriend to pick them up. Unless, of course, he doesn't care, which makes him an even bigger asshole than I previously thought."

"Well, this is embarrassing. Guess I need to plan my lies out better. Look, just go home, Quinn, so I can stop feeling completely humiliated and ashamed and forgotten . . . and, frankly, lost. I've been feeling so alone these past few months, I sometimes just want to hop on an eastbound train and ride the rails until I find a new existence." My hand flew to my mouth. "Wow, I'm pathetic. First I embarrass myself by getting caught in a lie and then I lay out a whole pity party spread. I'm not always this much of a downer. I'm just tired."

"You're never a downer. In fact, when I get to work and find out my favorite food server is not working, it ruins my whole night."

I flashed him one of those 'oh please' smiles. "As much as I would like to believe you—"

My words fell off as he took hold of my hand. "You don't have to but it's true." Even in the shadow of the building, his eyes were a vibrant green. "Now, let me give you a ride home because I'm not leaving you here alone. Another reason for me to hate what's his name. How dare he leave you sitting in the dark by yourself."

"Trust me, Quinn, you don't need to list reasons out loud for my sake. I've got a list a mile long. Anyhow, I'm not alone." I gazed up at him. "I'm with the Red Knight. And on that declaration—yes, a ride home would be nice."

Five

QUINN

My offer to give Suzy a ride had started out being one of pure chivalry. She was sitting alone outside a dark building, waiting for a ride that didn't seem to be coming. But just a few minutes driving with her, chatting about nothing in particular, listening to her lyrical laugh and watching her smooth the bottom of her dress down toward her knees a hundred times, I questioned my first motive of chivalry. Was I just doing the decent thing, or was I trying to find a way to spend more time alone with the woman who had caught my attention from the moment the boss first introduced us. I'd been so thrown off by my initial reaction to Suzy that I'd acted the idiot and jumped right into the *Suzy Q* song. For the past six months, I'd had to remind myself that she was with someone else but that hadn't kept me from making a valiant effort to flirt with her.

"Turn right here. I forgot to ask," she said after she pointed to the corner near her house, "how was Archer? Did he hurt his leg when he stumbled?" She laughed lightly. "By the way what a scare you gave the group of women who were out celebrating a thirtieth birthday. They were ready to race

27

out onto the field and administer first aid to the knight. Can't believe you stayed in the saddle with all that gear."

"That was more because Archer recovered fast enough to not dump me on the ground. Nick, the head horse trainer, walked him around for awhile. He didn't notice any lameness, but I think Archie earned himself a little well deserved R and R."

Suzy pointed ahead. "This is humiliating to say but it's the ramshackle little green house on the north side of the street. It's just a rental. I'm hoping to find something nicer—"

I put my hand on her arm. "Don't, Suzy. I know you work hard and cost of living is high." I pulled up to the curb and parked behind a red truck sitting in front of their house. Suzy's dented little car was parked in the driveway. A light was on in the front room.

"That's great," she said. "He's just sitting at home watching television and he still forgot me. Doesn't that make me feel special. Hopefully, it just means he's passed out from too much—" Her voice trailed off as the front door opened and a woman walked out onto the crumbling stoop. The porch light was broken but we could still see that she was carrying her high heeled shoes in her hand as she tiptoed over the dead grass.

My Porsche caught her attention. The woman completely ignored Suzy sitting in the passenger seat as she tucked her hair behind her ear and flashed me a smile before climbing into the truck and driving away.

We sat in awkward silence for a few seconds.

"Guess I know why he forgot to pick me up." There was no waver in her tone. "I wonder how long he's been seeing her." she said quietly.

"Knew that guy was a fuckface the second I met him." I looked over at her but she stared straight ahead. "I'd be glad to go inside and throw that jerk out on his ass. In fact, I wouldn't just be glad, I'd be over the moon happy to do it."

Suzy shook her head. "No, he's not worth the effort. Guess I'm not worth the effort either."

"Not true. Come home with me tonight." I rushed to explain myself before she could look askance at my offer. "I've got a spare bedroom . . . and a giant soak tub and a stocked wet bar. You could sit in a hot bubble bath, sip a glass of wine and forget all about the asshole inside that house."

She breathed in a long, deep breath. "Sounds better than sleeping on a park bench or, for that matter, inside that crappy little house with—what did you call him—fuckface?"

"Among other things," I admitted.

She nodded weakly. There was the slightest smile on her lips, but I knew, deep down, she was hurting. "I like fuckface. It suits him." She looked over at me. "Considering I haven't had a hot bubble bath since I was living with my parents, I'll take you up on your generous offer. But only for tonight. I'm just going to push all this shit out of my head for one night and pretend I'm in a different life altogether. Then tomorrow I'll figure out how to get that beer guzzling cockroach out of my house."

Six

SUZY

Since Quinn drove an expensive car, I expected him to have a nice place, but, in my mind, a nice place was a two to three bedroom house with a cute front yard of flowers and grass and a brick chimney. I might have heard tidbits about his beautiful house from those in the know, namely coworkers who had dated him, but I never expected a modern architectural masterpiece tucked in the side of a hill with full length windows overlooking the city.

As the car climbed the long, snaky driveway, I glanced over at Quinn. "This is all starting to feel surreal, like maybe I *did* just land in a different life. I'm sitting next to the Red Knight, who, by the way, looks just as dashing without the armor, and it feels like we're driving up to a castle."

Quinn laughed. "Not exactly a castle, but trust me, after my childhood, I sometimes still have to pinch myself when I'm driving up to this place. Of course, it's all courtesy of my brother, Trey. He's always looked after me. Even when we were growing up. Our single mom had to work three jobs to keep a roof over our heads. We had a few places that made your rental house look like the aforementioned castle. Trey was sort of a big brother slash dad. He missed out on a lot of stuff because of his baby brother." It was nice to hear him talk so openly and fondly about his brother.

A shiny black garage door lifted and Quinn pulled the car inside. There was a nice Toyota truck next to the Porsche's spot.

"Your garage is bigger and nicer than my whole house. I've got to ask—why do you work at the dinner theater?"

"Trey insists I work, and I'm glad he makes me. It keeps me busy and sane. He wants me to work for the Plaything Company, but I'd rather do my own thing. Plus, he's a big brother and he's kind of bossy." He climbed out and was quickly at my door to open it.

As I lowered my leg, I brushed my tender hip against the edge of the seat and winced at the pain.

Quinn offered me his hand. "That's the second time I've seen you scrunch up that cute little nose when something pressed against your hip. Did you hurt yourself?"

"Yes, it's just a bruise," I said, quickly, wanting to change the subject. Not just because it was too embarrassing to tell the real story but for the next twelve hours, before the sun broke in the sky, I wanted to pretend that Tate Silva didn't exist. On the drive to Quinn's hilltop home, I searched through my brain to see if there were any clues I'd missed about the woman in the red truck. I couldn't think of any, other than the general lack of affection between us for the past few months. But that was more on my side than his. Maybe he decided to look elsewhere for that attention. That was fine by me, as long as I never had to be touched, kissed or even looked at by Tate again.

We headed inside and entered immediately into a kitchen that was a steel, glass and stone confection. The furnishings were modern, sleek and masculine, but the thing that caught my interest the most was the view. I walked straight through a living room that was lined with soft leather couches and up to the large picture window that stretched from ceiling to floor.

In the background, I heard Quinn moving around glasses and popping a cork. Glittering city lights stretched all the way to the coast where the luminescent glow shifted into a shadowy gray. "How far are we from the ocean?" I asked. "Can you see it during the day?" I was talking loudly so that my voice would carry to wherever Quinn was in the house.

"Only at night." His deep voice, directly behind, caused me to startle. I spun around. He smiled as he held up a glass of wine. He had opened a beer for himself.

I took the glass of wine. I was no wine expert but it was definitely not the bargain stuff we served at work.

"We're about fifty miles and a few thousand feet up from the ocean in this house." He stood next to me to enjoy the view. "I can only see it when the city lights come on."

I sipped some more wine, suddenly feeling like I needed something to dull my senses and take the edge off. "This is the good stuff, eh?" I asked.

"To be honest, I'm not sure. Georgie, Trey's girlfriend, brought it over a few weeks ago, but she never got around to opening it."

I lowered the glass. "I hope it's all right that I'm drinking it."

"Sure is. Georgie would be happy to be giving her wine for a good cause. How are you doing after that unfortunate scene at your house?"

"I'm sure it will hit me like a category five hurricane tomorrow, but I'm determined not to think about it at all tonight." I lifted my glass. "Here's to Georgie and her great taste in wine."

"That sounds like a good plan." Quinn clinked his bottle

against my glass, and we drank while watching the city below vibrate and glow.

I was a lightweight when it came to drinking, and the wine was already relaxing me. "Hmm, I don't want to seem pushy or spoiled, but I believe there was mention of a bubble bath."

"Absolutely. You stay right here, relax and make yourself comfortable. I'll start the bath. This is your night to be pampered, and I plan to make it unforgettable." Quinn walked up to a panel on the wall. He tapped a button and music thrummed soothingly down from overhead speakers. He disappeared down a hallway.

I spent no more than two seconds asking myself what the hell I was doing in Quinn's house, drinking wine and waiting for a bubble bath. I couldn't count how many times I'd told myself that Quinn Armstrong was like that last piece of chocolate cake, rich, decadent and satisfying but you'd hate yourself in the morning. But tonight, I needed this sliver of fantasy. I needed to forget everything.

My phone rang in my purse, quickly shattering my goal to forget. It seemed Tate was finished with his fun for the evening. I pulled it out, my hands shaking and my face heating with anger. I was going to tell him to move out of the house and drop dead, preferably in that order. Then the flowery scent of luxurious bubbles floated toward me from the hallway and the fragrance swept me back out of reality and into my temporary fantasy. The last thing I wanted to do was screw it up by talking to Tate. Just hearing his voice would ruin the nice wine buzz in my head and the future bubble soak. I glanced at the phone, saw his name on the screen and promptly declined the call, then turned off my phone.

Quinn emerged from the hallway. "This way, milady. Your bubble bath awaits you."

I followed him down the hallway. "This probably sounds weird but I feel like a little kid going down the stairs on Christmas morning. Can't believe I'm this excited about a bath. I can't believe I'm saying all this out loud. Must be the expensive wine. I've only ever had cheap wine buzzes, and they aren't all that fun."

We reached a door. Quinn pushed it open to reveal an amazing white porcelain tub, deep and long enough to submerge myself completely. It sat in front of a large picture window with a view that matched the front windows in the living room. The geometric chrome light fixture dangling from the center of the ceiling had been dimmed to a perfect warm glow and three tall pillar candles had been lit and set on the corners of the tub. Iridescent mounds of bubbles were just starting to float up and off the surface of the water, dancing to the music that floated out of the speakers above.

I turned to Quinn. He looked extra heartbreaking under the dim, romantic lights. "If I don't come back out of this bathroom, tell everyone at work I died doing what I loved best, soaking in a bubble bath."

His deep laugh only added to the amazing ambience. "I will let you soak then. Do you want another glass of wine to sip?"

"Oh my gosh, you've got this spoiling a woman thing down to an art. But you know what, I'm already feeling pleasantly tingly from the first glass. I'm just going to submerge myself in those bubbles and get lost in a satisfying delirium."

Quinn bowed and walked out of the room, shutting the door behind him. I wasted no time taking off my work costume. I dropped the wide corset belt on the dressing bench and pushed the peasant blouse off my shoulders. The dress puddled at my feet. I took off my bra and pushed my panties down with just enough force to remind me of the bruise on my hip. I stepped out of the dress and walked to one of the two big mirrors over the double sink vanity. I had to hop up on tiptoes to get a clear view of my hip.

"Holy shit," I muttered. The dark blue and purple bruise had spread over my hip and down to my upper thigh. It was far worse than I'd imagined.

A light knock was followed by the door opening. I gasped as Quinn popped his face around the corner. He pulled it back out. "I'm so sorry," he said through the crack. "I thought you'd be in the water." Then his face peered around the door again and his gaze went straight to the bruise. "Jeezus, Suzy, what the hell happened?"

I picked up a towel and held it in front of me. Not that it mattered since he had seen every inch of me now. "It's all right, Quinn. You can come in."

He stepped around the door holding a silky blue robe. He had changed into jeans and a white t-shirt that fit so snugly across his chest I could see every muscle. "I was just bringing you a robe to put on after the bath." He was silent as he walked slowly toward me. I was suddenly aware of just how naked I was and just how much I wanted to live out that fantasy of being Quinn Armstrong's for one night, even if it was just for one night. It had just moved to the top of my things to do before I die list, one night of wild abandon with the Red Knight.

His breathing seemed to grow more shallow as he lifted his hand toward my hip. His fingers lightly brushed the tender skin but instead of pain, I felt a comforting warmth. It might have come more from his solemn expression, an expression that seemed to show genuine concern. It had been so long since I'd seen it in a man's face, I nearly forgot what it felt like to have someone care. How could I have stayed with Tate this long? What a fool I'd been.

"Midnight Oil." Quinn's deep voice mingled with the sound of rushing water.

I peered up at him in question.

"This month's subscription box from Plaything is called Midnight Oil. Lots of fun lotions and lubes, but the star attraction is a small bottle of CBD oil. I think it will help ease the tenderness."

"I've heard that stuff is good for pain." I slowly lowered the towel. I wanted to give him a clear signal that I wanted this, that I wanted him. He dragged his gaze away from the bruise on my hip to my breasts. My nipples hardened instantly.

His throat moved with a hard swallow as his heated green gaze stroked along my naked body to my pussy. He took a sharp breath and pulled his eyes back up to my face. "I'll bring you the oil. You can put it on after your bath." He walked out as if a fire-breathing dragon was close on his heels.

My shoulders slumped in disappointment. I'd made a point of dropping my towel to let him know I was up for a night of fun, but apparently, I didn't make the cut. He had slept his way through the entire female staff at work, but it seemed he had found the one woman he could say no to.

It was yet another stunning moment of embarrassment in a long, embarrassing night. Thank goodness I didn't force myself on him or throw my arms around his neck for a kiss. Although, the towel drop was humiliating enough, I supposed.

The billowing mounds of bubbles and fragrant steam weren't nearly as inviting now as I shuffled dejectedly toward the bath. I turned off the spigot and climbed inside, sinking myself down as deep as I could go in my pillowy quilt of bubbles.

Seven

QUINN

I paced outside the bathroom a few times with the bottle of oil clutched so tightly in my hand, I half-expected it to shatter. I needed to recover from seeing Suzy naked. It was a vision I'd imagined more times than would be considered decent. Still, the sight of her standing naked in my bathroom made my pulse race, her pert tits staring up at me with rosy pink nipples, the seductive curve of her waist, the waist I badly wanted to hold tight as I thrust into her again and again, the sweet little triangle of neatly trimmed curls at the top of her thighs. And those thighs. How often I had thought about being pressed between those thighs.

My heart rate had slowed some and my raging erection was fading. The water had stopped running so I counted on her to be completely covered by bubbles. For a second, the dropped towel had sent me mixed messages, and I nearly took it as an invitation. Then, I worried it was more of a test. Suzy already had a shitty opinion of me and my indiscriminate dating life. The last thing I needed to do was deepen that impression by throwing myself at her. She'd had a bad night and I'd invited her to my place with a promise of pampering and relaxation so she could forget about that asshole she lived with.

I took another deep breath and opened the bathroom door. All I could see was the top of her auburn hair over the mounds of bubbles. I relaxed some, thinking I could get in and out of the bathroom with my self-control and dignity intact.

"I'll just put the oil here on the counter," I said quietly.

The water sloshed and she popped her face up above the bubbles. "Oh, I didn't hear you come in."

"Sorry I interrupted your soak. I'll leave the oil here." I was making a quick, cowardly exit, something not normally in my nature but then nothing about my feelings for Suzy were normal.

"Quinn," she called softly from the bathtub.

I turned back. "Did you change your mind about the wine?"

"No, I was just wondering—At the risk of humiliating myself yet again, do you mind staying? I thought we could talk. We're both always so busy, we never get much chance to chat at work."

I hesitated only out of self-preservation. Sitting across from the tub, watching her bare shoulders rise above the bubbles, knowing that her luscious body was naked, soapy and wet beneath the surface was going to take more self-control than I had.

"That's all right. It's a silly suggestion. I'm sure you're not the least bit interested in a friendly chat or hanging around while I soak in this tub. You know, I think I might just call an Uber after this. My mom lives just twenty miles from here and—"

I walked over and sat down on the bench. "I don't want you to leave," I said with probably too much force. "I promise I won't touch you. I'm not here to seduce you. I just wanted to take care of you tonight. You looked so miserable sitting alone in the dark and so lost when you saw that woman walking out of your house . . ." My words trailed off, and I held my breath as she lifted onto her knees. She had tied her hair up in a loose knot showing off her long, slender neck. How fucking badly I wanted to trail hot kisses over her flawless skin. The silvery bubbles fell away from her breasts leaving silky wet skin and taut rose nipples.

If this was another test, I was sorely about to fail. I swallowed and was just about to speak when her lips parted.

"What if I want to be seduced, Quinn? What if it's exactly what I need tonight?" Her plump lips turned down slightly. "Though, I'd understand if you aren't interest—"

I crossed the floor in one long step. I reached down and took hold of her arms and lifted her to her feet. Bubbles and water dripped everywhere as I picked her up in my arms. I grabbed a towel on the way out of the bathroom. My heart pounded louder than my determined footsteps in the hallway.

Suzy rested her head against me as I carried her to my bedroom, leaving a trail of bathwater along the way. "And here I thought you didn't want me," she mused as I held her tightly against me, soaking my shirt with soapy water.

"That's on you, Suzy Q, because for the past six months, I've made it clear as day that there is nothing I want more. You just didn't believe me." I tapped the bedroom door with my toe and it swung open.

She trembled slightly as she peered up at me. I kissed her gently. The harder, deeper kisses would come later. Something told me Suzy was the kind of woman who wanted to be seduced slow and easy but fucked with wild passion.

"I could hold you like this, naked and wet in my arms for the rest of the night, but as much as I'd like to think that the tremble in your body is from me holding you, something tells me it has more to do with your wet skin and the cool air in this room."

She reached up and ran her fingers over the stubble on my jaw. "A mixture of both, I think."

I lowered her feet to the ground and opened up the towel. Just like earlier when I'd covered her shoulders with my coat, I wrapped the soft plush towel around her. I rubbed my hands over her back and shoulders.

"Hmm," she sighed. "This is what I call truly being pampered. And this towel." She rubbed her hand over it. "It's like being dried off with a warm, fluffy cloud."

She sucked in a breath as I knelt down in front of her. I patted dry her legs but quickly tossed away the towel. I wrapped my hands around her ass and brought her pussy hard against my mouth. Suzy tangled her fingers in my long hair, holding me harder against her. Soft, mewling sounds cascaded over me as my tongue pushed between the folds of her pussy to the magic button.

"Quinn," she whispered as she spread her feet wider to expose herself more. My hands gripped her ass, and she sucked in a sharp breath. In my fog of wanting her, I'd forgotten about the terrible bruise on her hip. I relaxed my grip but still held her firmly against my probing tongue. She gripped my hair and held my head to keep my mouth against her.

With just my mouth, I brought her quickly to a shuddering climax. Her fingers wound tightly around my hair and her groans of pleasure rolled down over my back. Her knees seemed to weaken as I licked away the last few waves of pleasure.

I pushed to my feet. Her long lashes fluttered at the end of heavy lids and a pink blush covered her skin. Once again I lifted her into my arms.

She rested her head against my chest. "A girl could get

used to being carried around in these arms," she said drowsily.

I lowered her down on my bed, taking care not to press against her sore hip. She stretched and sighed in comfort. "Oh my gosh, your bed quilt is even softer than the towel." She stared up at me as I loomed over the bed, taking pure fucking pleasure in seeing her stretched out on my blanket.

"Aren't you going to get undressed?" she asked.

I knew my answer before she asked it. I shook my head. "This night is for you, Suzy Q. I'm going to show you what it's like to be loved, adored and admired."

"I believe all those words mean essentially the same thing, but I'm fine with any one of them." She chuckled lightly as she sat up on the bed. She reached back and pulled the knot out of her hair. It cascaded over her shoulders and tickled the tops of her breasts. "It's been awhile since I've been adored or admired."

"That is where you are wrong. Now relax back against those pillows. I'll be right back."

I practically skated to the bathroom for the CBD oil. I hurried back to the bedroom, all the while reminding myself that this wasn't the night. It was going to take every ounce of my self-control but tonight wasn't for me. I wanted her badly, so badly that I was sure I wouldn't think straight. But her hip was sore and what she needed tonight was tender loving care. And I planned to give her plenty of it.

I stepped into my bedroom and smiled at the woman reclining against my pillows. She looked so perfectly right in my bed.

I held up the oil. "Let's start the pamper session, milady."

Eight

SUZY

It was only my hip and some soothing oil rubbed on the terribly tender reminder of my night, but it warmed me to the core. Quinn had brought me so easily to climax with just his tongue, I could only imagine what he would be like in the full throes of passion.

His hand moved past the bruise. He gently nudged me to turn onto my stomach where he spread the silky oil over my ass. The bed moved under his weight as he moved his knees closer and leaned down over me.

"I think this might help you relax." His voice rolled over me as a soft blindfold covered my eyes.

Instinctively, I reached for the blindfold. It was a new experience. I was trying to decide if I was experiencing excitement or fright. Quinn took hold of my wrist and moved my hand away from the blindfold.

His mouth pressed against my ear. "Trust me, Suzy Q," he whispered. I'd made up my mind. It was excitement that was made more intense by a sliver of fright.

Quinn pushed my hair away and kissed the back of my neck, sending a shiver of delight through my entire body.

"Hmm, I think I found a magic spot to kiss." His deep voice drifted over me like a warm blanket. He kissed the back of my neck again, then planted a long trail of hot kisses down my back. His hands massaged the oil into my skin. As he smoothed it over my ass cheeks, he lowered his mouth to kiss each one.

Moisture pooled between my legs. All I could think about was having him yank me to my knees to take me right then. The damn bruise on my hip seemed to be holding him back. Then my erotic wish seemed to come true. He pushed a pillow under me lifting my ass high in the air.

"Please, Quinn, I want this." How easily I'd slipped past reasonable thought and into pleading, but his hands and mouth had once again made me delirious with need.

Blindfolded, I rested my face against the pillow. My fingers gripped the sheets and I listened intently for pants to be unbuttoned, a condom package to rip open, some kind of sign that I would soon find that anticipated explosive release. The mattress moved and lifted. Footsteps padded across the floor. I waited for the sound of clothes dropping to the floor but it never came.

The footsteps neared again. Curiosity made me reach for the blindfold, but he took hold of my wrist before I could lift it. A tiny buzzing sound followed. I lifted my head from the pillow but didn't take off the blindfold.

"Relax, milady, this special toy came in this month's subscription box and now I've found the perfect use for it." He pressed the heavily lubricated vibrator against my ass first to ease me into the feel of it.

I startled at first. He leaned over and kissed my back to relax me. My body melted into the soft quilt, but my fingers still clutched it in anticipation. My pussy ached for attention. I lifted my ass higher in invitation.

His mouth moved down to my ass again and he kissed and

bit my skin as he slid the vibrator along the crack and down between my legs. I moved my thighs wider and pushed my knees forward, my throbbing pussy searching, waiting and begging for attention. The slick round tip gently gyrated against the folds of my pussy. I cried out in relief as Quinn slid the vibrator into me. A small vibrating protrusion settled against my clit. A low moan rolled up from my chest as I clenched the vibrator inside of me.

"Do you like that, baby?" Quinn's low voice melted over me.

"Yes, fuck, yes," I sighed into the pillow.

He leaned back down and his mouth pressed against my ass. His tongue flicked against the tight puckered hole. I clutched at the quilt, first stunned and then pleased at the intrusion. I had never experienced anything so intimate. I'd never been the center, the entire focal point of the pleasure. I was loving every damn second of it.

I drifted in and out of a dizzying warmth, a warmth that covered my entire body inside and out, then, suddenly, I found myself focused on one thing, the vibrating pleasure between my legs. I writhed against the vibrator as it tickled my clit and pressed against a tender spot deep inside that pushed me instantly over the edge.

Moans of pleasure pulsed from my lips as my body splintered into a million glorious pieces. Quinn did not stop his tender tongue caresses or pull the vibrator from my pussy until every shuddering wave had passed.

I was already stretched out on a soft quilt, but I managed to relax even more and melt into its pillowy comfort. Every inch of me, from the top of my head to my toes, felt lusciously satisfied. I no longer had a care in the world. It was just my naked body, the dreamy quilt and the even dreamier man whose mouth was still pressing warm kisses against my skin.

I reached up and lifted away the blindfold, peering back at him over my shoulder. "You, sir, deserve knighthood."

Nine

QUINN

I hadn't taken my clothes off or even had the pleasure of feeling Suzy's writhing hot body in my grasp, yet I felt amazingly content. The earlier despair was gone from her pretty face and she was wearing that million dollar smile.

I climbed onto the bed and sat next to her, leaning against my headboard. I reached over and pulled the edge of the quilt up to wrap her in its cocoon of downy warmth. She turned and moved so that her head rested on my lap. I stroked her silky hair. It still took all my willpower not to touch all of her.

"That was super-tacular," she mused. "Which is a new word I made up because what I just experienced deserves an entirely new term."

I smiled down at her as I caressed her bare shoulder. "I'm glad my efforts were worth a new word. I have to admit, I was sort of making things up as I went. The end result was a success."

"More than a success." She rolled her head to peer up at me. Just the tiny movement stirred my cock. "Seriously, Quinn, thank you for tonight. You managed to make a truly terrible evening turn out like a wondrous fantasy. Reality will return in the morning but at least I have tonight."

"Damn that morning reality shit," I said. "Suzy, one question. Feel free to ignore it but I'm going to ask it anyhow."

"Sure, go ahead."

"Did fuckface give you that bruise?" My muscles tensed as I waited for her answer. I had already envisioned myself dragging the asshole out to the front lawn to give him a proper pounding when the woman walked out of their house, but if he had physically abused Suzy, I was ready to destroy the jerk.

Suzy hesitated just long enough to push adrenaline through me. I couldn't believe how badly I wanted to hurt the guy if he'd laid one angry hand on her.

"Technically, he caused it but he didn't hit me. I would never have stayed with him if he hit me. As it is, I keep asking myself why I stayed with him this long."

I relaxed my jaw but wasn't thoroughly rid of the vision of pounding the guy into ground meat.

Suzy seemed to sense the tension seeping out of me. She pushed up to sitting, keeping herself rolled in my quilt. "It may not always seem like it, but I do know how to take care of myself."

I put my arm around her shoulder. "I know. I guess I was just looking for a reason to hurt fuckface. Just sounded satisfying."

She nestled close to me. "It sure does. But let's drop this subject. I'm in my fantasy zone, remember? And what you did to me a few minutes ago was pure, unadulterated erotic fantasy. The only thing that could make it better would be a hot fudge sundae as a finale."

I laughed. "Well then, we need that damn finale. You're in luck. I hosted the gang for a barbecue a few weeks ago, and by gang I mean my brother and his friends and their girlfriends. I told people to bring dessert and every damn person brought ice cream. It was my fault for not coordinating it better, but long story short, my freezer is packed with ice cream that never got eaten."

I got up and went to my dresser. I pulled out one of my t-shirts and held it up. "I think this'll work."

I walked back over to the bed. Sex looked good on her. Her cheeks were pink and her long hair was ruffled enough to make her look extra adorable. I handed her the t-shirt. "Put this on and follow me to the refrigerator."

After a good five minutes of decision making, Suzy settled on a bowl of caramel swirl ice cream topped with hot fudge sauce. We'd carried our sundaes out onto the back deck where a ceiling of stars provided light and a summer breeze carried the scent from the surrounding grass and trees.

"Fantasy complete," she said as she licked a drop of ice cream off her bottom lip, a gesture that made my pulse race. She put her spoon down and rested back against the patio chair. The movement caused the shirt to cling to her body. Her taut nipples pressed against the cotton fabric. Knowing it was my shirt that was lathing across her breasts and naked skin made my cock harden. "What about you, Quinn? What is one of your fantasies? Or maybe you wake up every day and live a fantasy." She waved her arm around. "I mean this place is incredible."

I put my bowl on the ground next to my lounge. "It is. I wish I could figure out a way to repay my brother but I don't know how you can repay someone who has given you everything. Which brings me back to my fantasy." I looked over at her. "I was always the little brother, my mom's youngest. It seemed everyone was always taking care of me, looking out for me. I want that. I want someone in my life who I can take care of, someone to look after. I'm surrounded by loving friends, who I also consider family. But I want that one special person who is solely connected to me." I knew damn well I was looking at the person who already fit my description, but Suzy had never shown any interest in me. She was always sweet and friendly and fun, but she had never given even the slightest hint that she would want me in her life. I couldn't blame her. She considered me a player. I pretty much deserved that title.

Suzy tilted her head side to side. "I have to admit, that is not the fantasy I expected from the Red Knight."

"Well, before you hand me some kind of scout badge for gentlemanly manners, I should finish. Of course one of my prerequisites for this special person is that she loves sex and wild foreplay and is open to adventure in the bedroom."

"Ah ha, see, that's more what I expected out of the notorious Quinn Armstrong."

"Thought I would lead with the scout stuff hoping it would make me sound better." I stood up and lowered my hand for her to take.

"At least you earned a badge for honesty." She patted her mouth to stifle a yawn before placing her hand in mine. "I think your prerequisite sounds fun. I particularly like the wild foreplay part."

"See, I thought you might say that. I'm always telling myself, I'll bet that Suzy Q is someone who likes to have fun."

I led her inside. It was well past two in the morning.

"I'm going to let you have my bedroom, and I'm going to crash in the guest room." The words sounded stranger than hell as I said them, but I wasn't going to blow it by sleeping next to her. There was no way I'd be able to get through an entire night without fucking her. She was just too damn hot.

"No, I couldn't put you out like that. I'll take the guest room." She pressed her knuckles to her lips to stifle another yawn. "I'm so tired, I could lay down on your kitchen floor and fall into a deep sleep."

"No, take my room. I insist." I walked her down the

hallway and stopped at my bedroom door. It felt as I was walking her to her parents' door. I was even a little nervous about the kiss goodnight. But there was no fucking way I was going to walk away, shut myself into the guest room, and climb into the cold, lonely bed without at least a taste of her lips.

We stopped outside the door. She peered up at me with her extraordinary eyes. "Thank you for everything, Quinn. I feel surprisingly calm and not altogether unhappy about the ugly crap I'm going to have to face in the very near future. That's all because of you."

"It has been my pleasure." I leaned down and kissed her, gently at first, then deeper. My tongue swept against hers, and she pressed against me dropping her head back, inviting me to kiss her longer. But I'd already taken my willpower to its limits. I didn't trust myself. This night needed to end like this, with her feeling better about her circumstances, and, with any luck, her thinking better of me. It would be hard to erase the reputation of a bed hopping scoundrel, but hopefully she was able to get a glimpse of the other side of Quinn Armstrong.

It took every ounce of my self control to pull my lips from hers. She crumpled lightly against me as if I had drawn away her breath by ending the kiss.

A glimmer of disappointment crossed her face but she forced a smile. "Thanks again. I can't wait to burrow in that quilt and fall fast asleep. Good night, milord."

"Good night, milady."

Ten
SUZY

As expected, I slept thoroughly and soundly. I opened my eyes to a midday sun. I sat straight up and glanced at the clock. It was nearly noon. I needed to get home. I needed to leave the fantasy and head back into the bleak reality that was my life. I'd worked hard not to think about Tate so as not to ruin the delicious night I'd spent with Quinn. He had behaved so differently than I expected that I was more than a little surprised and pleased. Perhaps I'd let rumors and coworkers' bragging have too much sway in forming my opinion of the man. Maybe he wasn't the player they all made him out to be.

I lowered my feet to the floor. The house was quiet. It was entirely plausible that Quinn was still sleeping. We had stayed up through half the night and that was after a long shift at work. For a terrible moment, I let myself wonder what my night would have been like if Quinn hadn't found me sitting on the bench. I would have had no choice except to walk to the station and ride the horrid public bus, which, after midnight, was occupied with the strangest people. Worst of all, I would have walked into my house, ready to chew Tate out for forgetting me only to find that he was fucking some woman. God, had they fucked in our bedroom? In my powder blue sheets?

I kicked the awful thoughts from my mind. I headed into the master bath, another manly but sumptuous retreat like the bathroom with the soak tub. Straight sharp lines of glass and tile were interrupted by the occasional chrome fixture. Since my overnight stay was unplanned, I would have no choice except to pull back on my costume slash serving uniform.

I washed my face and swirled a dab of toothpaste around my mouth for a few minutes. I stared at the bedraggled looking reflection in the mirror and made some quick tucks and smooth outs of my hair. It was going to have to do. As I fussed with my hair and wiped mascara out from under my eyes, a phone beeped somewhere behind me.

I spun around and noticed Quinn's phone was sitting on the dressing bench between the shower and second vanity. I had no right to look at it but my curious gaze swept over the screen. It was a text from someone named Zoe. "Are we hooking up tonight or not?" That was all the text read. It was a pretty straight forward question, so it didn't require a lot of words. There was no one named Zoe on the work staff so this particular friend was someone outside of the dinner theater.

I laughed quietly but the sound of it echoed off the tile walls. "You silly woman, Suzy," I said to myself. "You knew he was a player. One night of pampering didn't mean a darn thing." I had almost been convinced by his big heartfelt speech about wanting someone in his life to take care of, someone solely connected to him. It seemed there were probably more than a dozen women connected to him, and I was certain each one of them had been treated to a special fantastical night like me. It was probably his special trick, his pick up plan. And what an elaborate plan it was. I nearly fell for it, but I was going to give myself a little leeway on this one considering I had started the night being tossed into a coffee table and finished the night watching a woman trek out of my house with her high heels in hand.

Even so, I wasn't mad at Quinn. There was just something so genuine about the man, it was hard to dislike him. And I'd had one hell of a nice time. My pussy was going to ache every time I thought about it. Maybe all I needed was a subscription to Plaything and some of those magical toys.

I walked back into the bedroom. Quinn had delivered my work outfit and purse to the room. I pulled out my phone and turned it back on. There were three voicemails and two texts from Tate. I ignored all of them and called for an Uber ride. I remembered the street name but not the number on the house so I told them I would wait on the corner.

I changed back into my server's outfit. The smell of barbecued turkey legs and onion wafted up from the flimsy cotton material. I shoved the corset belt into my purse. I was going to look strange enough walking around in an off the shoulder peasant dress. I didn't need to freak out my driver more with a corset belt.

I was more than relieved that Quinn was still sleeping. I hurried and finished dressing, then walked out to the kitchen to search for a piece of paper and pen. There was a notepad and pen in one of the kitchen drawers. I pulled it out and wrote him a quick message.

Hey, Quinn, thanks for the fun night. It really helped. See you at work. Suzy

I decided to keep it brief and informal without any flirty embellishments. That was more for me than for him. He already knew last night was just one in a long line of one night stands, but I needed to reinforce that notion in my own head.

Otherwise, it would be pretty damn easy to get lost in the delirious, delicious idea of being Quinn's permanent lover.

I had gone to bed tired but also slightly disappointed that Quinn hadn't wanted to sleep with me, that he was happy to provide me with an awesome dose of pleasure but he didn't want to climb into bed with me. Now I was glad we hadn't been more intimate. It would have been much harder to accept never having his attention again after having him in bed. I was sure a long, naked, wild night of lovemaking with Quinn Armstrong was unforgettable. The last thing I needed right now was to have my head clouded with dizzying erotic daydreams of my time with him.

I walked quietly to the door. My quickly hatched plan of a fast, no strings escape was dashed. Unlike the shabby front door of my rental house, where the deadbolt no longer worked and the only thing keeping us from thieves and murderers was a thin, breakable chain, Quinn's front door was controlled by a keypad. Damn rich people and their fancy electronics.

I spun and around and looked toward the glass doors leading out to the deck. The same keypad security system controlled that door too. I startled when a door down the hallway opened. Quinn walked out wearing nothing but a pair of shorts. I'd caught glimpses of his naked chest when he was pulling on his tunic and armor in the dressing area, but I'd never had a full, unobstructed view. A tingle of heat swirled through me, and my heart did what I could only describe as a butterfly dance. He was male perfection from his broad shoulders down to the trail of dark hair that bisected his six pack. His hair was messy from a long morning of sleep, but it looked good on him.

His gaze dropped to the purse in my hand. "Were you sneaking out?" He smiled but there was a sprinkle of hurt in his tone.

"I think I've intruded on you long enough. I've called for a ride, so I'll be out of your hair in just a minute."

His face fell. "Out of my hair? Is that really what you think? Suzy, I enjoyed having you here. You are not intruding. I thought we'd make some lunch."

Every cell in my body was saying put down the purse, cancel the Uber and stay for lunch, but how the heck was I going to untangle my emotions from this mess once he grew bored and moved quickly on to his next houseguest. In fact, Zoe had plans with him tonight. I wouldn't even have a full twenty-four hours of being his *special* guest.

It took all my self-control to say no. "I think I need to go deal with—you know—fuckface. But I had a great time, and I'll see you around—at work."

Quinn raked some of his disheveled, long hair back with his fingers. The gesture revealed the black patch of hair under his arm and the bulging muscles of his pec and bicep. It was such a simple, natural movement, yet it sent my passion hormones into overdrive.

He padded on bare feet to the door. His silence could have been interpreted a million ways, but I was sure it was mostly relieved resignation. He knew just as well as me that we weren't going anywhere with this one night of semi-intimacy. It couldn't even have been summed up as a night of intimacy because it was one-sided.

"You're sure you don't need a ride somewhere?" he asked. "I could throw on some clothes and take you home. You might need me—" he paused, "you might need a friend when you confront that asshole."

I smiled weakly. "No, I need to face him alone. I'm not afraid of him. I'm just worried it won't be that easy to peel him off my couch and out of my house. Thanks again for everything, Quinn. You've been a great friend."

More disappointment swallowed his expression at the word *friend*, but it was the only word that made sense.

I walked outside into the warm afternoon sunshine. I glanced back. "By the way, your phone is in the bathroom in case you're looking for it."

"Thanks, I was wondering where I left it. Good bye, Suzy Q." He shut the door.

I headed down the long driveway to the road. There was an unexpected tug at my chest as if I had just walked away from something I would not soon forget.

Eleven

QUINN

Watching Suzy walk down the driveway and out of view, I reminded myself that I was chasing stars trying to catch someone like her. She had no interest and she'd made that undeniably clear with her hasty exit. Hell, she was even trying to sneak out, a move I had pulled more times than I liked to admit, when I wasn't interested in any subsequent conversation or relationship. But this time was different. This time she was sneaking out on me. Guess I now knew what a slap in the face it was to the person being snuck out on. Jeez, I was a fuckface too.

I headed into the bathroom to retrieve my phone. I walked through the bedroom. Suzy had made the bed and smoothed the quilt, but I could still see the impression her head had left on my pillow. The t-shirt I'd leant her was folded up and sitting on the foot of the bed. Something told me I wasn't going to wash the shirt anytime soon. I was that close. I had Suzy in my bed, tucked beneath my quilt, even wearing my t-shirt, but she had fled the scene, anxious to get away from the notorious player.

I picked my phone up off the counter. There were three

texts, including the first one that was from Zoe about hanging out tonight. It had come through earlier, while Suzy was still here. She made a point of telling me about the phone, which meant she had absolutely seen it sitting on the counter. Since I'd never taken the step of hiding my texts, I could easily assume Suzy read Zoe's text. Zoe was a woman I occasionally hung out with. She was a lawyer and she was constantly traveling. Whenever she was in town, we made plans to meet up. Although our meet ups were basically a good dinner out followed by a long night of fucking. Then she would pick up her expensive suit jacket and her thousand dollar high heels, blow me a kiss and head out the door. I wouldn't see her again until her next stop through town and even then, occasionally, we were both too busy to make it work. Today, I wasn't feeling it. I also had a good excuse. I was still covering for the pickle jar disaster. The show would not go on without the Red Knight.

I texted her back. "Sorry sweets, I'm working tonight."

She texted right back, unusual for her. She must have been feeling extra horny. "How am I gonna keep myself busy without my favorite fuck?"

"I'm sure you'll figure something out," I replied. Normally I would have been bummed that I was too busy to hook up with Zoe, but this morning, I was glad to have an excuse.

I was working hard to convince myself that my lack of enthusiasm to see Zoe had nothing to do with the angel who just walked out of my house. But if I was being honest with myself, I didn't need to analyze too much. For months, I'd been wanting to get closer to Suzy, to find out why I was so darn obsessed with her, to prove to myself it was only because she was taken and I couldn't have her. But after the asshole she lived with hammered a nail in his own coffin last night, it seemed Suzy was no longer bound to a boyfriend. Yet, I was still thinking about her nonstop, her smile, the smell of her hair, the curve of her neck and an ass that was just asking to be kissed, pinched and spanked.

I put down the phone and walked to the shower. I turned on the water and flicked the lever to cold. I was definitely not over my obsession with Suzy Q.

Twelve

SUZY

I felt close to nauseous as I climbed out of the Uber car and headed to my front door. The television was on so I knew Tate was home. Where else would he be? The bigger question was would he be alone? As I pondered that question, I realized I didn't give a damn either way. I just wanted him out of my life. Any connection or feelings I'd felt for the man had been completely wiped away by the sight of the woman carrying her shoes across the front yard. And if I really thought about it, most of those feelings had been thin and fragile at best. I had slowly lost my interest and affection for Tate, and last night was just the push I needed to sever our relationship for good. That old cliché you're better off without him could not have been more true.

On the drive home, I'd sorted through the other emotions I was experiencing, the ones that were centered around Quinn. He actually seemed somewhat hurt that I was leaving, or, more accurately, sneaking out on him. For a fleeting moment, I'd allowed myself to dream that it was because he actually cared. I flipped back through all my encounters with him at work and all the times he'd insisted he was waiting for me to be free of Tate. On one occasion, when I teased him about seeing not one but two of my coworkers in the same day, he told me he was just filling time while he waited for me to come to my senses and realize I was meant to be with him and not Tate. Naturally, I always fluffed it off as flirting. He oozed charisma and confidence, and I was sure he told every girl the same darn thing, knowing full well that it would work. Only it had never worked on me. That was mostly because of Tate and my ridiculous scruples that would never have allowed me to cheat on him. But it was also because I didn't want to be one of Quinn's conquests. I didn't want to be added to a long list of women who drifted in and out of his life, stopping for some amazing sex and leaving with a good dose of heartbreak on the way out the door. I had come to the solid conclusion that I had made the right decision by heading out the door before anything more could happen. And after my time in his bedroom, with his mouth on me as he brought me to climax still fresh in my mind . . . and body . . . I was sure it wouldn't take much for me to be tempted right back into his bed.

My hand was shaky as I jammed the key in the lock. The door swung open before I could turn it. My key flew out of my hand along with the door handle. Tate was shirtless. I briefly did a comparison with the last shirtless man I saw and realized Tate had gotten soft and flabby in his time off work. He had dark rings under his eyes but I somehow doubted that had anything to do with him waiting up all night for me to come home.

"What the fuck, Suzy? You've been gone all damn night. Why weren't you answering my calls? I was trying to let you know I was on my way to pick you up from work."

"Oh really? Did you drive over to the dinner theater to

look for me?" I pushed past him and put my purse down. Even though it was past noon, I was in desperate need of a cup of coffee.

He never answered my question. I scooped coffee into the basket and switched on the pot, then turned around and leaned against the counter with arms crossed. "Since you haven't answered, I can only assume you never bothered to look for me."

Tate walked into the tiny kitchen leaving little room between us. A look of contrition crossed his face. "Well, you didn't answer my calls or texts so I assumed one of your coworkers was going to give you a ride home."

I reached for my favorite coffee cup, the one with the panda bear. "Yes, as a matter of fact a coworker gave me a ride home—" I left a dramatic pause to make certain he heard the rest of my statement. "To his place."

His expression turned into stone. "What the hell do you mean *his* place?"

The coffee maker beeped. I took my time pouring myself a cup while he breathed loud and hot like a dragon shooting fire through his nostrils.

I took a sip of coffee, sighed and secretly marveled at how calmly I was handling this whole shitty thing. It was most likely because I had already resolved myself to this relationship being dead and over long before I reached the front door.

"Hmm good stuff," I said about the coffee. "I figured since you were entertaining another woman here at the house, I could *do* what I like. And I like my coworker."

The cold, hard expression sagged into stunned guilt. "What the hell are you talking about? I wasn't entertaining anyone, and who the fuck is this coworker? It's that fucking big shot with the Porsche. The asshole never takes his eyes off you. I caught him staring at you at the picnic, and I think it's time the two of us go toe to toe."

I was startled to learn not so much that Quinn was always looking at me, I'd caught him occasionally gazing across a room at me or smiling over heads at me, but what I found hard to believe was that Tate had actually taken notice, that he had actually felt a surge of jealousy about it.

I pulled myself back into the conversation and looked directly and confidently at him. It was amazing how unattractive he'd become to me. "I don't have to tell you anything about my private life because we are through. You and I are no longer connected in any way. Since I've been paying the rent on this place, you need to pack your shit and get out. Preferably by the time I get home from work tonight. That gives you over twelve hours. I think that's being generous with time."

A short, dry laugh spurted from his mouth. "I'm not going anywhere." He turned and walked out of the kitchen. I'd been prepared for that exact reaction.

"Then I'll pack my stuff right now." I carried my coffee cup out of the kitchen.

"Fine with me." He plopped on the couch and held up the remote to change channels. "The house is in your name, so they'll be coming after you when the rent isn't paid," he said smugly.

I stopped at the couch and seriously considered pouring hot coffee over his head, but I held back that urge. "Yes, it's in my name, and on the way home just now, I called the landlord and gave our thirty day notice. The house is paid until then, so I guess, once again I'm being overly generous because you don't deserve anything but a kick in the ass. Seems you'll have no choice except to find a job. Or maybe you could move back with your lovely mother, the tarantula queen." I leaned over the couch. "By the way, if you went toe to toe with him, you'd be wearing your couch sitting ass on your head."

"Fuck you, whore," he barked as I walked down the hallway to the bedroom, feeling at least a smidge of satisfaction. Now, if I could just figure out where the hell I was going to stay while I sorted out my life.

Thirteen

QUINN

Archer's big muzzle tickled my palm as he plucked the carrot from my hand. The Friesian was on stall rest for a week after his stumble in the theater arena. Since I had been the rider on his back, I felt somewhat responsible for his injury so I'd brought a five pound bag of carrots to work. The horse didn't seem to mind being on stall rest, especially when it meant fresh carrots.

It had been an endless night of choreographed jousting, and I was glad it was over. I planned to head home, get mildly drunk and watch movies until my inebriation pulled me into a deep sleep. Suzy and I managed to successfully avoid each other, which helped stave off any awkwardness between us. I really hated the idea of awkwardness when it came to Suzy. It meant our friendship would be strained. Even if I couldn't have her in my life, the way I wanted, I hoped we could remain friends.

The horses were housed in nicely built stalls that jutted off the back of the massive restaurant theater. I circled around the building to the parking lot. Most everyone had gone home for the night. The parking lot was empty except for the horse trainer's truck, my Porsche and Suzy's little, beat up sedan. I looked back toward the exit. There were a few lights on near the rear of the building.

I could just get in my car and drive off. She had a car this time so she had a ride home. But what if fuckface had refused to move out? Some friend I was. I'd been avoiding her all night, when I should have sought her out to make sure she was all right. When she left my house this morning, taking a little sliver of my heart with her, she was heading home to confront her awful boyfriend. I'd seen the bruise on her hip. She claimed he was responsible but that he hadn't hit her. He was, without question, an asshole.

It wasn't like her to be staying late alone. I headed back around to enter through the barn area where the trainer was checking on the animals before going home. It was the easiest way back through to the main area of the building where the employee locker rooms were located.

The jousting and dinner arena looked giant when it was empty. I crossed the arena and headed through the door that would take me to the locker room. Light glowed through the small window on the women's locker room door. I peered through the glass. Suzy was sitting on the bench with a sweater pulled on over a light blue sundress. She rested her feet on a large duffle bag as she texted someone on her phone.

I didn't want to startle her by barging into the room so I tapped lightly on the window. Her face popped up. It took her a second to recognize the big face peering through the glass. Her smile was my invitation to open the door.

I popped my head inside. "Is the coast clear?"

"Just me sitting here," she said. "The other girls have all gone home. Anyone in particular you were looking for?"

Her question deflated my shoulders. "You, Suzy, I was looking for you. I know that's impossible for you to imagine, but I came here to find you. I saw your car and I wanted to make sure you were all right." None of the expected awkwardness materialized, but there was still more tension between us than before, back when I was just the guy who dated way too many of her coworkers and she was the girl who I admired from afar, waiting and hoping that someday she would come to her senses and leave her boyfriend. In that scenario, she dropped fuckface and came running to my open arms. Only I'd blown it by being just as much of a fuckface as Tate. Although I wasn't as big a jerk. Or at least I sure as hell hoped not.

She lifted her phone. "Just waiting to hear back from a friend. I'm hoping I can camp out on her couch a few days until I get my life straightened out." There was a good dose of sadness in her pale blue eyes. I hated to see it. "You were avoiding me tonight," she said quietly.

"No, not really," I countered lamely.

"You always make a point of carving out a few minutes to see me whenever we work the same shift. No matter how busy and hectic things are, you always stop by to say hello or give me a wilted daisy you plucked from someone's garden or a chocolate donut you saved from breakfast."

I smiled and shook my head. "My gosh, no wonder I haven't wooed you. What a fucking dork I am bringing you daisies and donuts." I pointed at her. "Although, that one donut I brought you last week had sprinkles, so there's that."

"And I enjoyed every last sprinkle on my break." She stood up and took a deep breath. "I'm glad you're not avoiding me altogether. I would hate to think we can no longer talk after our night together."

"I was hoping the same thing. I'm sorry about all of it, Suzy. I'm sorry I'm such a fucking disappointment. I deserve every negative thought you have about me."

She placed her hand on my arm. Her fingers were long and

soft and warm. "No negative thoughts," she said as she lowered her hand. "Only positive ones."

She stooped down to pick up her duffle. I shot my arm forward to take hold of the handle. My hand wrapped temporarily around hers and it seemed charges of electricity circled our fingers. I knew I was holding the hand of the woman I'd been wanting since I first met her. Unfortunately, she didn't see me in the same light.

"I can carry the duffle out to your car." I lifted it. "Feels like you have your whole life in here."

We headed through the dark building to the parking lot.

"Pretty much my whole life. Which shows you just how pathetic that life is. The good news is that the bruise on my hip is less tender, so I was able to sling pints of ale without too much problem."

"Your life is not pathetic." I stopped in the dark hallway and turned to her. It was a narrow passage and due to my size we were nearly pressed against each other. My typical thoughts went right to a vision of me pushing her up against the wall and sliding my hands underneath the sundress. My cock pushed against the fly of my jeans as I tried to shake the image from my head.

I knew I was pushing myself to the limit but I took hold of her hand and kissed it. "Milady, you are far from pathetic. You are stunning and smart and funny and the sexiest damn woman I have ever met. And if I was a different person, a stranger just meeting you for the first time, I would use that chance to start over and show you just how much I could love you."

Her eyes were glassy as if she was close to tears. She'd had an emotional twenty-four hours and looked ready to fall into a million pieces. She pressed her hands against my chest, a move that was meant to be casual but it set my pulse racing. "And if you were a different person I wouldn't like you nearly as much. You should never change for someone else, Quinn. I just learned that the hard way. I went out of my way to bend to what Tate wanted in a girlfriend. Somewhere along the way, I lost myself. But I'm determined to find the original Suzy again."

In her own gentle way, she was telling me that she wanted to be left alone. I couldn't blame her. It sucked big time but I was going to respect her wishes. I peeled away from facing her. I could swear I heard the snap of static electricity as our auras separated. Or maybe I was only hearing that on my side.

As we headed across the parking lot to her car, her phone beeped. She pulled it out and looked at it. "Shoot. My friend has her sister in town so there's no couch. As you probably surmised, I moved out, instead of Tate. I did give the landlord notice though, so with any luck, fuckface will find himself out on the street." She sighed. "Guess I'll be heading to my mom's after all. Oh boy is she going to grill me seven ways to Sunday about my breakup with Tate."

I laughed. "I thought it was six ways to Sunday."

"Not with my mom. Seven is being conservative. On the bright side, there will be a heaping plate of pancakes waiting for me when I go downstairs in the morning."

"Not sure if it's a trade off for the grilling," I said, "but it can't hurt."

We reached her car. She spun around to face me before opening the door. "I'm glad things didn't get tense between us, Quinn. I would have missed this."

That's because we have something special. That's why I want to be with you, is what I wanted to say. Instead, I just nodded and smiled and told her to pop the trunk for her duffle bag. There was no way to deny that I was feeling past miserable about the reality that Suzy just didn't have romantic feelings for me. It was my first time on the other side of being hurt, and I was starting to feel pretty damn shitty about myself and the women I'd hurt. It seemed it was time for me to find myself too.

I placed the duffle in her trunk. It was filled with boxes sealed with tape. I shut the trunk. She worked hard to put a roof over her head and now she had to give it up to the jerk. He never deserved her in the first place.

"Thanks for carrying my bag." She smiled up at me from the driver's seat.

"Anytime. And if you get sick of pancakes, you have a room at my house. No strings attached, I promise."

She gazed up at me and a faint smile appeared. Her smile was always punctuated with one dimple on her right cheek. It was just one of the incredible details I'd memorized about her.

"That's nice to know." She pulled her leg into the car and I shut the door. I walked to my car. Headlights lit up the lot as Suzy turned her car toward the exit. Mildly drunk or not, I was going to have a hard time not thinking about her tonight.

Fourteen

SUZY

I reached a stoplight and took a few aggravating seconds to search for my mom's house key. It was attached to an old Mickey Mouse key chain. I'd left it on the key chain to remind myself that going home meant that, like a little kid, I couldn't hack it on my own. I tried more than once to convince myself that my new status of being homeless was not my fault. I had a house, crummy as it was, that was paid for all the way through next month. But I really had only myself to blame. I'd stuck with Tate for a good year longer than I should have. Somehow, I'd talked myself into being in love with him, but my feelings for Tate had turned around so sharply, I couldn't even think about standing in the same room with him, let alone sleeping in the same bed. As far as I was concerned, that chapter of my life was so completely over, it was as if months had already passed since I first saw the woman leaving our house and since I told him we were through.

My fingers brushed over the cold metal Mickey Mouse key chain. I yanked it free of my purse and stared at it. After being out on my own for three years, I was heading back to my pink and white little girl bedroom. Mom was, no doubt, going to recite a long list of mistakes I'd made in the past three years that led to my humiliating downfall.

I dropped the key in the console and cranked up the radio, hoping it would lift me out of my grim mood. I had no idea what the odds were that the first song playing would be CCR's *Suzy Q*, but they would have won me a nice payoff in Vegas. There was no way to not think about Quinn, on his first day of work, when he belted out a few verses of the song upon meeting me. All I could think was—wow, this guy is as confident as he is good looking. And his singing voice wasn't bad either. We became instant friends because of that unique first meeting. And, just as I'd mentioned to him tonight, after our initial introduction he always made a point of searching me out, even if it was just to say hello. He never missed a chance to talk. "Never," I said quietly beneath the din of the music.

I pulled into the left lane and headed back the way I'd come. It was stupid and crazy and I was absolutely, definitely going to regret this in the morning. But my life was just out of sync enough that a little impulsiveness was easily excused. At least that was the argument I was going to tell myself after the full weight of regret sank in. But how much regret could there be. It was Quinn Armstrong, after all.

I had expected to be a bundle of nerves and indecision as I turned onto the road that would eventually lead me to the top of the hill where Quinn's extraordinary house was nestled in the hillside, but surprisingly, I felt quite calm. That was until the notion set in that Quinn might have invited one of his many *friends* over to spend the night. Wasn't Zoe asking about hanging out?

I drove up the long driveway. The garage was closed, and there were no spare cars parked out front. For all of five seconds, I considered turning back around and leaving.

"Damn it, Suzy, grow a pair. Just go up to the door and knock. What's the worst that could happen? An incredibly gorgeous woman could answer dressed in skimpy lingerie. That's the worst, I think. It certainly wouldn't be a shocking surprise. Then I could just apologize and slink away to my pink and white room and pile of pancakes. So stop talking to yourself and do this, Suzy."

I climbed out of the car. Motion lights went on over the front porch, illuminating the entire front yard. I hurried to the front steps. I had never done anything like this, but I was going to go for it. Hopefully, a leggy blonde in a skimpy nightie wouldn't answer the door.

I rang the bell. There was a long enough pause that I quickly drummed up an image of Quinn being yanked out of a moment of passion by his front doorbell. He would just ignore it then, wouldn't he? God, I hoped he would ignore it. I considered knocking but talked myself out of it. He wasn't coming to the door. I'd psyched myself up for nothing.

I was just about to turn around when the front door opened. He was wearing only a pair of low slung shorts on his hips and no shirt or shoes. He looked like a giant package of heartbreak, but I'd come this far . . .

"Every time," I said, with a slightly hoarse throat from the nerves, "No matter what was happening, or how busy we were, I could count on hearing that clank-y armor and those big black riding boots coming down the hall to the serving station. I guess because I'm me and well you"—I clumsily waved his direction—"well, you are *you*, and let me tell you, you really are spectacular from head to toe. I couldn't let myself even think there was anything there. I thought you were just being nice but then I thought about *every time*. You really have searched me out every shift with your daisies and donuts, and now that I'm standing here babbling like a loon, you'll probably wish you hadn't brought me those wilted—"

His hand shot out to stop my ridiculous speech (thank goodness). The door snapped shut behind me as I slammed against his hard, unyielding body. I threw my arms around his neck. His mouth pressed down on mine as his hands slid down my waist and beneath the hem of my dress. His large palms cupped my ass and he lifted me up so my pussy was pressed against him. I wrapped my legs around his waist wanting nothing more than to feel the hard heat of his taut muscles rubbing against my aching pussy.

He pulled his mouth free for a moment. "Do you have extra panties in that duffle?" he asked. There was an unusual grainy quality to his tone, as if every muscle in his body was stretched tight.

"I don't just have this one pair, if that's what you're asking." I said lightly.

There was a tug on my panties and the sound of fabric ripping followed. I wasn't sure, logistically, how he managed it, but my panties fell away from my body.

I blinked up at him. "You're like some kind of panty magician."

"It's a gift."

"I could have just slid them off," I suggested.

"Sorry, milady, that's not the knight's way. We stick to an entirely different code of chivalry." He swung around with me clinging to him like a koala on a tree and carried me down the long, dark hallway.

His tongue explored my mouth as his hands held my ass firmly in his grasp. "I can't." He groaned against my mouth. I pulled my mouth from his and fought back tears of disappointment.

"You don't want me?" I asked, my voice sounding thin and raspy in the empty hallway.

"Are you fucking kidding?" He turned me and lowered my feet to the floor. "I just can't make it to the bedroom."

I glanced down the hallway to his bedroom. "It's literally right there," I noted but the fevered glaze of hunger in his eyes assured me those extra five feet were like a mile.

Quinn pushed the sweater off my shoulders. I felt the soft fabric brush the backs of my legs as it fell to the ground.

In seconds, I was sandwiched between the cold plaster wall and his hot, hard body. He kissed me in a way that would surely leave my lips swollen and bruised. He pulled the hem of my dress up. His mouth lifted from mine and he gazed with deep green eyes at my face and lips.

"Is anything wrong?" I asked quietly.

"Just making sure you want this." His voice was low and strained from arousal.

I responded by lifting my mouth back to his and reaching for the button on his shorts. They were loose enough on his hips that one button and they slid down to his ankles. His hard cock brushed against my hand. A groan rolled up from his throat as I wrapped my fingers around his erection.

I pulled my mouth from his with a slight gasp at the size of it. This time it was him to ask the question.

"Is there anything wrong?" he asked as he continued a trail of kisses along my neck.

"On the contrary, everything is fucking magnificent," I whispered against his ear. I stroked him, taking in the full length of him. Hot moisture surged between my legs at the thought of him thrusting into me.

Another long stroke coaxed hot beads of sticky moisture from the tip of his cock. I rubbed my thumb around it, thinking about how delicious the sticky fluid would feel against my pussy. My teasing was too much for him.

He growled and took my face between his hands. "I have never wanted anything so badly—" He stepped out of his shorts, then paused. "Fuck."

"Oh my gosh, now what?" I asked with a certain degree of

frustration. "I, too, have never wanted anything so badly. I'm so close to orgasm a waft of cool air between my legs might just trigger it."

"Sorry, I'm usually much smoother, Suzy Q, but you've got me spinning." He swung me around and carried me to the bedroom.

"Guess you decided that the bedroom wasn't too far after all. Kind of relieved because I really do love that quilt of yours."

"Yeah, and my condoms are in the nightstand. Didn't think it would be too cool to leave you pantiless in the dark hallway while I roll on a shield."

"Good thinking." I nuzzled his neck as he carried me to the bed. He smelled like soap and dreamy man.

He dropped me in the center of the quilt.

My hands smoothed over it. "Ah, my old friend, Mr. Quilt." I rolled over onto my stomach and propped up on my forearms. My feet danced in the air and I watched with undivided attention as he rolled the condom over his incredible cock. I couldn't stop a mewling sound from rising in my throat at the thought of him inside of me. He caught the sound and didn't try too hard to suppress a cocky smile.

"Were you surprised to see me at your door?" I asked.

"Surprised"—he climbed onto the bed, naked and erect and turned me onto my back—"and fucking pleased as punch." He lowered his face to mine and kissed me, gently this time, a stark contrast to the more punishing kisses just a few minutes earlier. I liked the gentle kisses just as much. "Seriously, Suzy, you've got me spinning. I don't want to fuck this up."

I smoothed my hands over his shoulder and back, feeling each curve and ridge of muscle. Just touching his naked skin rekindled the craving I was feeling in the hallway. "I'm not breakable or special, Quinn," I said as I smoothed my hands over his ass. "There's no way you can fuck this up."

He moved his kisses down to my breasts. I arched my back against the feel of his tongue as it lathed my nipples. As he kissed and suckled each breast his hand moved down, along my stomach to my pussy. His fingers left a hot trail on my skin and between the folds of my pussy as he teased my clit.

"Fuck yeah," he groaned as his finger slid into the sticky moisture pooling in my pussy.

I reached for his hair and tugged it slightly. "Quinn, I'm so close. I'm nearly over the edge and I want you to be inside of me when I fall."

He shook his head beneath my grasp. "Don't you dare come until I'm inside of you. I want to feel your pussy clench around my cock," he commanded gently but continued to fuck me with his fingers. He leaned down, brought his mouth to my pussy and flicked his tongue against my clit.

I released his hair and clutched the sheets. "I'm not going to be able to stop," I cried.

"Not yet, baby. I have to feel and taste you for a minute longer. Don't come yet. Don't you dare come," he teased with words and with his tongue and fingers.

"Quinn," I said on a breath, "I don't know if I can stop it. Please."

He lifted his tongue away from my clit long enough to gently bite the inside of my thigh. Not expecting it, I sucked in a shocked breath.

He grinned up at me from between my legs. "There, did that take you back from the brink?" He returned his tongue to my clit and plunged his finger deeper.

I tangled my fingers through his hair. My body convulsed with tension as I tried to keep back from the edge. "Quinn, fuck me please. I need you now."

He removed his fingers and positioned himself over me. I clutched at his arms, no doubt leaving fingerprints in his skin. His mouth covered mine, but I was so delirious with arousal I could hardly focus on the kiss. A cry of anticipation flew out of me as his big hands wrapped around my ass. He pushed my pussy higher as he settled snugly between my thighs.

His groan was low and deep, like a growl as he slid inside of me. My pussy instantly tightened and clenched around his massive erection. Waves of pleasure pulsed through me as Quinn pumped into me, faster and harder with each thrust. I gripped him with my legs, wanting more and more of him, as much as he could give.

The muscles of his arms tensed and his long, hard body followed as he pushed into me again. His groan circled the room and floated over me, filling me with emotion, an emotion I'd never felt with Tate. He would finish and I would slip out from under him and discretely turn away. But I wanted nothing more than to stay beneath Quinn, his cock buried firmly inside of me, for the rest of the night. That thought made my chest ache. I had to remind myself that the wonderful naked man in my arms and intimately connected to me at that moment was Quinn Armstrong. I'd known full well, as I approached his door this evening, that I was going to be making myself vulnerable and risking heartbreak by starting something with Quinn. It would be fantastic and fleeting, and it was going to take a long time to forget the feel of his arms around me, his hands and mouth on me, but I was going to have to face that cold reality. Given his history, that time would come sooner than later.

But in the meantime I was going to enjoy every damn minute of it and try not to think about the hurt that was sure to come afterward.

Fifteen

QUINN

I rolled over and reached for Suzy but found an empty bed. I covered my eyes with my arm to shield them from the daylight seeping around the blinds. I searched around the bedroom. It was empty. I shot straight up to sitting and was instantly relieved when I saw Suzy's sundress hanging over a chair. The smell of coffee brewing and eggs cooking pried me from the bed.

I had woken her three times through the night, finding it impossible to sleep soundly with her naked in the bed next to me. Just as I predicted, I couldn't get enough of her, and frankly, I was feeling pretty renewed as I stepped out of bed. I grabbed a condom from the nightstand and marched toward the kitchen with purpose.

Suzy was wearing one of my t-shirts, like she wore her first night with me. Her long legs jutted out from beneath the hem as she stood at the stove stirring the eggs. She glanced back over her shoulder when she heard my footsteps.

"Hope you don't mind that I cooked some breakfast," she said as she turned back to the stove.

I reached her and turned off the stove.

"Hey," she protested and then laughed as I picked her up in my arms and put her down on the opposite counter.

"You're wearing my shirt," I muttered through my kiss on her neck.

"And you're not wearing a damn thing." Her voice softened and became raspy as she relaxed in my grasp. She placed her hands back against the counter and pushed her ass closer to the edge. "Quinn," she said on a sharp breath as I dropped to my knees in front of the counter and rested her legs over my shoulders.

I reached around her ass and pulled her hard against my mouth. She chirped excitedly as I drove my tongue into her to taste every bit of her sweetness. I gazed up at her as my mouth worked its magic. There was nothing fucking better than Suzy in a dizzying state of arousal. Her head dropped back as she braced herself on her hands. Her long lashes fluttered down and her mouth parted, begging to be kissed, just like her pussy. She contracted her ass to push her pussy tighter against my mouth. I responded by pushing my tongue farther into her, my face smothering against the hot folds and her taut clit. She writhed against the feel of my mouth on her. Every time she moved, silently begging for more, my cock grew harder than rock.

"Oh, Quinn, fuck yeah." She lifted her ass nearly off the counter allowing my tongue to penetrate every inch of her. The soft, drowsy moans coming from her throat were too much. I continued my attention to her pussy

She groaned as I lowered her legs and pulled my mouth from her pussy. She opened her eyes, her lips parted first with disappointment and then with anticipation as I settled myself between her legs. Her hands stuttered across the counter and she gasped as I yanked her forward. Her head dropped back again as I pushed my throbbing cock into her. She wrapped her legs around my waist, and I drove my cock deeper.

Her arms nearly collapsed behind her as her eyes drifted shut. I reached forward with one hand and pushed the t-shirt up above her breasts. I needed to see all of her. I drove in with long, sweeping thrusts.

"I can't get enough of you, baby," I growled as I moved my hips and contracted my ass. I wanted to reach her very core, to let her know that I planned to stay there buried inside of her forever.

A pink blush covered her skin and her nipples tightened to tiny hard buds as her cries of pleasure floated around the kitchen. Her pussy clenched around me, milking me to an orgasm. I continued to pummel her, not wanting the sensations to ever end. Her arms grew too weak to hold herself up against my thrusts. She kept her legs wrapped around me and threw her arms around my neck as her body shuddered and writhed with ecstasy.

As the waves slowed, she crumpled against me. I tightened my arms around her. "Now about that breakfast," I said as I kissed her forehead.

She pulled back and peered up at me. Her pale blue eyes were slowly becoming a permanent fixture in my mind. "Worked up an appetite, have ya?" she quipped.

"I'll say." I gripped her closer. "And she's a saucy little wench to be sure."

Sixteen

SUZY

I'd heard him entering my dining station. It was impossible not to. But I still startled when his arm snaked around my waist. His armor breast plate pressed against me as he kissed the back of my neck. "I love the way you keep the hair up off your neck. Gives me easy access."

"I hate to let you down but I actually keep it up for food sanitation reasons. Not to lure rogue knights into kissing me." I rested my head back, forgetting temporarily that he was covered with metal. I pulled my head forward and rubbed it. "I think I prefer you in the flesh instead of armor." He released his hold on me. I glanced around to make sure no one had seen him kiss my neck. My coworkers were all busy in their own stations, hurrying to get ready for the boisterous crowds about to sweep into the dining areas.

Quinn caught me looking around. "So you've made your mind up," he said. "You're not going to tell anyone about us?" There was a small edge of hurt in his tone.

"First of all, the last thing I want is angry, jealous glares from my coworkers. I also don't want to be trading bedroom stories with any of them."

His face dropped with a slight look of shame. "Good point."

"Plus, we've only been seeing each other for three weeks. This is so new and to be honest, I'm still reeling about it all. Which is partly due to the non-stop mind-blowing sex but it's also because I came right off a long term relationship and I landed straight in your arms."

He took my hand, glanced around and planted a kiss on the back of it. "That's because these arms have been open and waiting for a long time, waiting for you to see that you belong to me."

I stared up at him, unable to hide my feelings. He slowly released my hand. "Did I say something wrong?" he asked.

"No, not really. I want to be yours, Quinn. If you truly mean it, but I don't want to be *owned*. I realize I've let myself be that person before, never questioning anything Tate said or did. I don't want that. I just want to be loved, unconditionally and forever."

This time he didn't make sure the coast was clear. He took hold of my face and leaned down to kiss me. "I can do that, Suzy Q. I promise," he whispered against my mouth.

His words sounded genuine. They sent a deep curl of hope through me but I needed to stay on guard. I couldn't lose myself to this man yet. There were too many variables, too many cautions to give in to the overwhelming sense of connection I was feeling for Quinn. I knew if I didn't keep my wits about me, I could lose myself to a world of disappointment and heartbreak. And I was in too fragile of a state to let that happen.

I reached up and placed my palm on the side of his face. I wasn't ready to respond to his promise so I switched topics. "If I don't get these pints of ale ready, the diners in the Yellow Knight's section might throw me into the jousting ring."

His mouth turned down for a second, assuring me that he

was disappointed in my non-response. Then his magnetic smile returned. "And just how did milady end up rooting for the yellow knight, my sworn enemy, this fair evening?"

"Good sir, you know how excited I get when you talk like a knight." I pressed my body against his, but it was so coated in layers of costume it was a lost attempt at flirtation.

"Then I must say ado"—he bowed—"and wait until later this evening when I can talk dirty in my knight-speak."

I laughed. "Can't wait for that. Not quite sure how that will sound."

He nodded. "That makes two of us." He leaned closer. The scent of his soap was already becoming familiar. It triggered a surge of tingles in my pussy. "Doth—spreadeth thine thighs, milady work?"

I laughed again. "Not sure if ending every word in th is exactly considered medieval English."

"Then I suppose—I will fucketh you until you screameth my good name—is a no go."

I pushed at his chest. With the armor it was like pushing against a brick wall. "Be gone, Red Knight, so I can get my friggin' work done."

"See you later, Suzy Q . . . preferably naked." He turned around in his unwieldy costume and tromped out of my station in his heavy riding boots.

Seventeen

SUZY

"Are you cool with a little bedroom adventure?" Quinn asked as he stepped out of the shower.

I patted my face dry to rid myself of the sticky scent of medieval dining fare and all around work odor. We had rushed home after work, barely able to keep our hands to ourselves on the entire drive home. I was especially glad Quinn had been behind the wheel and not me when he reached across the console and put his hand under my peasant dress. He deftly managed to make me come without even removing my panties. It probably helped that I'd stayed in a permanent state of arousal as I watched him ride around the jousting arena on his fine black steed. He truly fit the bill of the breathtaking, brave knight with his long hair and finely chiseled jaw. After all the months of watching him perform, admiring him from afar, squelching a bit of jealousy knowing that other women had the pleasure of being seduced by the tall, dark Red Knight, I was thrilled knowing that I would be the woman in his bed for the night. And hopefully many nights after.

I put the towel down and allowed myself the pleasure of

watching him dry off his naked body. Every inch of him was spectacular. "What exactly do you mean by adventure?" I asked.

He walked over and circled his wet towel around me to draw me against his body. His cock was already pushing at the t-shirt I'd pulled on. I had grown fond of wearing his oversized t-shirts after work. They were comfortable and they smelled of his soap.

"I've got a few tricks up my sleeve. Or have you forgotten my family connections to Plaything, 'your pleasure is our business'?"

I leaned forward and licked a drip of water off his chest. "How could I forget when I've been on the receiving end of some of their wonderful lotions and toys. I'm tired from my shift, but I think I could manage energy for a little adventure."

"That's the spirit." He tossed the towel onto the dressing bench and grabbed my hand. I had to hurry my pace to keep up with his long strides as he led me out of the bathroom and across his vast bedroom.

"Lose the t-shirt, milady," he ordered as he walked to the panel in his room that would adjust the lights to a warm romantic glow and usher music from the mostly hidden sound system. He glanced back at me just as I reached for the hem of the shirt. "Hmm, what music should we set our adventure to? Is there any singer whose voice makes you hot and horny, Suzy Q?"

"Well, now that you ask, Eddie Vedder," I said quickly without having to give it any thought. Vedder had always been my favorite.

Quinn pushed a button and Counting Crows came on.

"That's not Pearl Jam," I noted.

"Nope. The last thing I want is for you to be dreaming about Eddie Vedder while I'm fucking you."

"Never took you as the jealous type," I quipped.

"Only when it comes to you, Suzy Q. Why the fuck are you not naked yet?" He stomped across the room to pull the t-shirt off. He lifted my chin and lowered his mouth for a gentle kiss.

"Where are these hidden tricks?" I asked. "Although, I must admit I could stand here in the center of this room and have you kiss me like that for the rest of the night, and I'd be happy with that. Eddie Vedder or not."

"Well, we can kiss in the center of my room another night." His long, muscular legs carried him across the room to the walk-in closet. He disappeared inside and emerged pushing out a large wedge with his foot. It was covered with soft gray leather and looked like something a person would use at the gym. Every sort of vision went through my head as I tried to figure out exactly what our adventure would entail.

I blinked up at him, innocently. I was certainly feeling it. "Are we going to be doing sit ups because I think you'll outperform me there with that six pack."

His mouth tilted cockily up on one side. "No sit ups tonight." He drew two fluffy pink cuffs out from behind his back with one hand and pulled out a satin blindfold and bottle of lotion with the other. "Are you ready?"

I took a deep, steadying breath and was suddenly thankful for the glass of wine I'd had when we got home from work. "I'm ready but I'd be lying if I said I wasn't a little nervous. Confession time, that blindfold and vibrator on my first night here was about the wildest thing I've ever done on a bed."

"Then this is perfect because we won't be on the bed." His voice trailed off and his gaze grew dark and green, a glazed look I'd seen before and one that sent a thrill through me. That look meant I was about to be taken to the height of passion by a man who could push me over the edge of an orgasm by just whispering dirty words in my ear.

Quinn's arms went around me and he pulled me against him. His cock pushed and nudged my belly, letting me know the adventure had started. His tongue probed my mouth, coaxing a soft mewling sound from my throat and a swirl of hot moisture through my pussy.

I was so lost in his deep kiss, I hadn't noticed the fuzzy cuffs going around my wrists until the last one snapped shut. Each cuff had a leather strap and a metal loop attached to it.

He peeled his hot, hard body away from mine and circled behind me to tie on the blindfold. I startled slightly as his mouth pressed against my shoulder and neck. "God, every damn inch of you is as sweet as sugar."

The silky blindfold made it impossible to see. I was at his mercy, which was exactly where I wanted to be. His warmth left my back and I sensed that he was circling around me again. My right arm lifted, and he tugged me gently forward by the leather strap.

I scooted my bare feet across his plush carpet. After a few steps my shins touched the side of the wedge. The leather was soft and supple against my skin.

"Get down on your knees, milady," Quinn muttered against my ear. "You are about to get the royal treatment."

A tiny squeak chirped from my lips. His soft chuckle drifted over me like warm fingertips as I lowered myself to my knees. The wedge was pressed against my thighs now.

Quinn tugged against on the leather tethers, both at the same time and a little harder than before.

"Oh," I squealed as I found myself leaning over the tall side of the wedge with my head at the bottom. My arms were being fastened to each side of the wedge, something that thrilled me and sent a slight shiver of fear through me.

Quinn, who never seemed to miss even the slightest reaction, placed a kiss on my jutting, naked bottom. "No need to worry, Suzy Q. I think you'll have a lot of fun on this adventure." He kissed my ass again and trailed his mouth along the back of my thigh.

My body relaxed as my pussy grew wet with desire. I dropped my head and rested my cheek against the soft leather, deciding to give in to the intense physical stimulation. He had proven himself such a master of my body, it was as if we had been together for years and not just weeks. It would be too easy to ruin the moment by allowing my thoughts to drift to the reason why he was such a master so I pushed them away. All my focus went to the cravings I was feeling, the intense need to be satisfied.

A splash of oil on my lower back made me jump slightly. Quinn chuckled again, then began smoothing the luxurious fragrant liquid over my back and bottom.

"Hmm," I said as I relaxed again. "Like the world's best massage. I like the feel of that lotion on my skin."

"It's from the Midnight Oil box. It's really popular. Lots of sweet hineys getting lotioned up this month." With that he delivered a sharp, tantalizing slap to my ass.

I jerked up but was instantly reminded that my hands were bound.

He spanked me again, but this time instead of startling and pulling against the cuffs, I groaned in pleasure and pushed my bottom higher. Surprising the hell out of myself.

He spanked me once more, then soothed my stinging flesh with more lotion. I sensed Quinn moving behind the wedge. He spread my legs wider with his knees as he settled in behind me.

"I have to say, I like this view a lot." His settled his mouth on the crack of my ass and leaned down to impale the tight hole with his tongue. I was both sensory deprived and on sensory overload. The intimacy of his pressing his tongue between my cheeks sent a new shiver of delight through me, one that he noticed immediately.

"You like that, baby," he growled from behind before continuing.

I was so focused on the ass play, it took me by surprise when his cock slid into my pussy. I cried out in pleasure, nearly delirious with the feel of his tongue and cock, both invading my most intimate spots.

"Quinn!" The intensely erotic position and his masterful skills took me easily over the edge. My body trembled and I writhed against him to feel every pulsating sensation. It seemed to last forever, each wave of pure pleasure rushing through me, making me dizzy and breathless.

"That's it, baby, that's what I wanted," he growled as his hands took firm hold of my hips. I collapsed over the wedge and clutched its edges to hold on as Quinn pummeled me hard from behind. Each thrust renewed some of the earlier sensations. I instinctively braced against his punishing thrusts just to feel them again. I was so out of my mind with it all, I hadn't realized that he had brought me right back to the cliff again. My pussy had hardly recovered from the first orgasm, but I was heading over the edge again.

Quinn sensed I was heading for another orgasm. He slowed his thrusts, keeping himself in check so that I could come again. He gave me a little spank. "Let's do this again, baby. I want a second act." He held me firmly against him with one hand and slipped the other down between my legs where his finger went to work teasing my clit. He strummed my magical nub like a maestro, with just enough pressure to bring me back to orgasm.

This time my cry of pleasure was weaker. Quinn had milked away all of my energy and I was merely a frail, trembling rag doll being filled with an explosion of sensations, "Quinn," I said weakly, blissfully as I again collapsed in a heap on the wedge.

Quinn's low groan filled the room as he once again

gripped me firmly with both hands. He slammed into me three times, his grasp on my hips getting stronger with each thrust. "Fuck, your pussy is so sweet," he growled as his body stiffened and he came.

He collapsed down over me, warming me like a big heavy blanket. He kissed the back of my shoulder. "I knew you were the adventurous type, Suzy Q."

"Hmm." A luxurious sigh hummed from my throat. "I had a great tour guide. And it turns out he doubles as a warm blanket."

His laugh tickled my neck. "I suppose we could move this to the real blankets."

"We could but I don't know if downy quilts have anything on your body heat."

"I never said anything about losing my body heat," he said as he peeled himself off of me. "Although, I have to say, I do love seeing you draped over this wedge, with that perfectly spankable ass sitting high in the air."

I wriggled my bottom with the bit of energy I had left.

He crawled around to the front of the wedge, pulled off my blindfold and released me from the cuffs. Before I could peel myself off the leather wedge, Quinn leaned down and plucked me into his arms. I relaxed against him, breathing in the scent of his skin as he carried me to his bed.

He lowered me onto the bed and pulled a quilt up over me. "I'm going to the kitchen to get us each a bowl of ice cream. Adventure night has made me hungry," he said.

"Wow, double orgasm and ice cream in bed? Please don't wake me. I want this dream to last forever." My body ached with sexual fatigue as I snuggled up under the lush quilt and drifted into a luxuriously drowsy state of bliss.

Eighteen

QUINN

Suzy and I sat on the deck, sipping margaritas and watching the sunset. We'd been dating only a month but I felt more at ease and happy with her than anyone else I'd ever met. We were instantly best friends and perfectly suited in bed, only confirming my initial feelings that we were made for each other. It was early and still tenuous, so early in the relationship that I hadn't dared mention it to my brother. He would be annoying me with fatherly lectures about not blowing it, and if it ended, then he'd never let me live it down. Our coworkers knew nothing either, even though we'd risked being caught more than once. That was mostly due to the fact that the Red Knight just couldn't seem to keep his hands off the pretty tavern maiden.

We'd both had the night off, a rarity. Normally, I would have been up for a night out at a club or dancing, but I'd discovered I didn't want to share Suzy with anyone. I wanted her all to myself, and since we both spent many hours in a crowded, noisy dinner theater, we were happy to stay home and order food in.

"My brother called earlier today. He's taking the *Plaything*

I out for a day on the water next weekend. Do you think you're ready to meet him?" Trey would expect me to bring a date but what he didn't know was that this wasn't just a date. This was the woman I'd been admiring for months. I would definitely have to prep him ahead of time so he wouldn't embarrass the hell out of me, a skill he had honed in his life-long role as my older brother.

Suzy twisted her pink lips in thought. "Not sure. That sounds kind of scary." She sat forward. "Wait, did you say *Plaything I*. Since it's on the water, I assume it's a boat. But does the one mean there are multiple *Playthings*?"

"Just two. What can I say, sex sells. A lot."

"Guess he certainly picked the right business. Seems kind of soon to meet the family but I'll give it some thought."

"It'll just be Trey and Georgie. I could make it really stressful and invite the whole darn gang," I suggested.

"Definitely not ready for the whole gang but I would like to me Trey and Georgie. If my work schedule permits, I think we can consider it a date." Suzy stretched her long legs out on the lounge and patted her stomach. "I hope the food arrives soon. I'm withering away with hunger."

I put my glass down next to the lounge and folded my arms behind my head. "I'm hungry too. Who knew a night in could burn so much energy?"

She turned her head to face me without lifting it from the lounge. "It might have been the three hour adventure session in the bedroom," she quipped. "I must admit, sex with you is like a few hours of exercise boot camp. It always leaves me exhausted, achy and extremely satisfied."

"As your personal trainer, I'm happy to help you meet those training goals." The doorbell echoed through the house. "Ah ha, nourishment has arrived. Which is good because we need calories for the next adventure." I lowered my feet to the ground.

Suzy sat up too and flashed her empty glass. "I'm going to head to the kitchen for a refill. Are you interested?"

"Nope, I'm good." I waved her past and into the house. We split off as she headed to the kitchen and I walked to the front door. I pulled it open, expecting a pimply faced kid holding two bags of food. Instead, Ginger and Ellie, two friends, strode right inside in tight mini skirts and high heels. Ginger was carrying a bottle of wine.

"We are tired of the new hermit style Quinn," she said as she waved around the bottle.

Ellie took my arm and started pulling me toward the kitchen. "We haven't seen you at the club for weeks so we decided to bring the party to you." Something behind me caught her attention. I didn't have to turn to know exactly who was standing behind me . . . with a look of pure hurt on her pretty face.

"Ginger, Ellie—" I pulled my arm free of Ellie's grasp. "This is Suzy."

"Fun, she can join the party," Ginger chirped. She cast a sly smile my way. "After all, what's that you always say? The more the merrier." She winked and poked my side. Ginger smiled at Ellie. "Though we've never gone past a threesome. Maybe tonight is the night."

"Actually, I was just leaving," Suzy said with a waver in her voice. "If you'll excuse me." She hurried past us. Once again I was freeing myself from Ellie's grasp.

I hurried after her.

"Quinn," Ginger called after me.

I glanced back. "It was nice seeing you both but if you could see yourselves out that would be great." I wasn't so much angry at their uninvited intrusion as I was at myself for living like a partying playboy for the last two years. It might have been fun at the time but now it was coming back to bite me in the ass big time.

I reached the bedroom and knocked lightly on my own door. I could hear Suzy sniffling as she rummaged through the drawers for her things. I opened the door.

"Suzy, they just showed up. I haven't seen them in months. I haven't seen any other woman since you came into my life. I swear. I haven't even so much as returned a text." Fuck, I sounded like a pathetic loser pleading for a lifeline. I sensed right away it wasn't working.

She swiped clumsily at her tears. "I don't blame your friends." She pushed her clothes into her duffle bag. "I blame myself. I don't know what I was thinking jumping into this. I'd just come out of bad relationship and then without thinking, I —"

"Jumped into another?" I asked, feeling about as hurt as she looked. "This isn't a bad relationship, Suzy Q. Far as I'm concerned, it's the start of something brilliant. I know I have a lot of baggage from my previous life but I swear I can change."

She struggled to close the zipper on her bag but got a shirt stuck in it. Then she struggled to open it. It wouldn't budge. She shoved the duffle away, sat on the bed and dropped her face into her hands.

I walked over and freed the fabric from the zipper, then sat next to her. "Don't give up on this, Suzy. Please."

She lowered her hands and turned to me with a pink nose and glassy blue eyes. "I think I just need to step back for awhile, Quinn. I was reeling from my breakup, then you swept in with all your knightly gallantry and those pecs. Damn those pecs. I just need some space. I need to just be me, with no strings attached, for awhile. I need to get my head straight. I can't do that around you because you have the opposite effect. You make my head spin." She placed her hand on my arm. "In a good way, mind you, but I think I need to take some time to clear my head."

She stood up from the bed. It felt as if a tether she had attached to my heart snapped in two. She was leaving me. Those were the only coherent words in my head and they were brutal.

"Where will you go?" I asked.

Suzy took a deep breath. "My mom's. For as long as I can take it, anyhow."

I picked up the duffle and carried it out of the room. There was no sense in me trying to make myself a fine, upstanding, gentleman. That ship had sailed. Hell, it had sailed and sunk at sea. Now I was losing the one woman who I was certain could be my port, my person to come home to.

We headed to the door. Thankfully, Ginger and Ellie, who were not always the sharpest, took the hint and cleared out. I opened the door. The food delivery guy was standing on the porch with dinner, just about to ring the bell. Our quiet, romantic night in had been blasted to pieces. I pulled a twenty out of my pocket and tipped the guy and told him he could have the food too. I knew my only dinner tonight was going to be a few beers and a long night in bed staring at the ceiling counting how many ways I deserved this.

The kid looked stunned, then shrugged as he headed back to his car with the bags of food. I walked Suzy to her car. I briefly considered not handing over the duffle but desperation never looked good on me. Even though I was feeling a good dose of it as I watched her open the trunk of her car. She avoided looking at me, and I was somewhat relieved. It was hard to look into her pale blue eyes and think I wasn't going to see them peering over the pillow at me in the morning. I'd grown way too used to having her next to me. The big bed was going to feel pretty fucking lonely without her.

I placed the duffle in the trunk. By the time I shut it, she was already climbing into the driver's seat for a quick getaway.

I grabbed the door to stop it from closing. It seemed to take all her will, but she finally lifted her face to peer up at me.

"Suzy, once you feel like your head is clear and you know what you want, I hope you'll come back to me."

She blinked away new tears and nodded as she pulled the door shut. I stood on the driveway, like a damn fool, watching, waiting and hoping she'd turn her shitty little car around. But she drove off, around the corner and out of sight. And out of my life.

Nineteen

SUZY

"Suzy," Gene, the assistant manager called over the radio at my station. "Time for your break."

Tonight was one of those nights where I couldn't wait to step away from the dining area. A party of twenty hyped up, drunken frat boys had landed in my section, the blue section for the night. It was always the luck of the draw, which server ended up with the most boisterous and rowdy crowd. Unfortunately, tonight I was the one with the short straw.

Down below, Peter, the jousting announcer, tooted his bugle and called out that the Red Knight had entered the arena. I'd learned a week after walking out on Quinn that he was an impossibly hard man to forget. The fact that we worked at the same place definitely didn't help matters. As hard as I tried not to, my gaze swept down to the jousting arena as the crowd in the red section cheered and whistled for their hero. He was still holding his helmet under his arm as he trotted Archer to the center of the field. His long hair was drawn back, away from his face. I could see his profile perfectly. I'd already memorized every line of it and seeing it made my throat ache.

Before I managed to pull my gaze away, he turned his face in the direction of my table section. Our gazes locked like magnets until I forced mine away. As I hurried to the door that would take me to the break room, one of the fraternity members, a thick necked idiot who had been handsy and rude all night, called to see where I was going.

"Hey, wench, where are you going? We need more ale."

I ignored him and rushed out the door to the break room. I had ten minutes of quiet and solitude which would hopefully give me enough time to recuperate from the last few seconds where Quinn and I locked gazes. We had both been expertly avoiding each other, not too big a challenge considering he spent most of his time on the side with the horses and theater team and I spent mine in the kitchen and dining areas.

I'd left his house that night, chastising myself for immediately falling head over heels for the guy when I knew he was a player. I blamed it on my vulnerable state of emotion, my breakup with Tate and losing my place to live. I was mostly sore about the last part. In fact, I'd hardly given Tate a second thought since I walked out on him. I was relieved to have him out of my life. But giving up my independence and moving right in with Quinn had been a big mistake. I was immediately dependent on another man, albeit a much better man than the first. Everything had moved with ridiculous lightning speed, and when the two women showed up, it was like a dose of reality. I asked myself what the hell I was doing moving right in with the guy. I'd cut off his busy social life and I'd cut off my own independence all with one stupid decision.

I checked my phone for the first time since my shift had started. There were two texts from my mom, one to remind me to lock the back door when I came in and the other to let me know she had washed the sheets on my bed. Mom had resisted learning to text for a long time but now that she used it, she found the most comically inane things to text about. But she had been there for me the night I came home from Quinn's. I spent a good hour sobbing into my pillow so she a baked my favorite lemon cupcakes. My mom always knew how to make things better with butter and sugar.

Brenda, one of the other servers, came in looking about as worn out as I felt. "Hey, Suzy," she said with low energy as she tromped to the employee refrigerator and pulled out a yogurt. Brenda had amazing curly blonde hair that she occasionally streaked with color. Tonight it was a wide swath of pink at the front. She had pulled the pink strand back and twisted it in with her gold hair.

She pulled out a chair and plopped down. "I've got the most irritating family sitting in my section tonight. 'Get me some more barbecue sauce please. Can I have another soda? This meat is too cold'," she said in a squeaky, annoying voice.

"I'll trade you the annoying family for my table of rude frat boys."

"Ugh, no thanks. They are usually the worst." She peeled open her yogurt. "Did you hear the terrible news?"

I sat up a little straighter. "No, please don't tell me they're cutting hours again."

Brenda looked up from her yogurt. "What? No, that wasn't the terrible news." She sat forward. "Are they cutting hours again?"

"Not that I know of, I just thought that might be your terrible news." I glanced at my phone. My break was almost over.

Brenda relaxed back with her lime yogurt. "No, that's not the news. Everyone is heartbroken. Quinn turned in his resignation." She shrugged. "Not sure why but he's probably going to work for that rich brother of his."

I blinked at her, trying to sort out my own feelings. They were pretty easy to sort. I was feeling despair. I would never see him again. "Is this certain or just a rumor?" I tried not to show how devastated I was by the news, but apparently, I wasn't doing a great job of masking my emotion.

"Jeez, are you all right?" Brenda asked. "You look kind of pale. Of all people, I didn't think you'd care one way or the other since you were one of the few women in the place he didn't date at one point or another. Although, I guess I saw you two talking occasionally."

"Yes, we were friends," I said weakly. I stood up from the chair but my legs were like jelly. Quinn was leaving. I'd never see him again. The weight of that reality sat on my chest like a lead ball as I willed my feet forward and headed back to my station.

The jousts were in full force down below the dining arena. It could just have been my dark mood but the noise echoing through the massive room seemed extra thunderous. The fraternity table had taken their enthusiasm and noise level up a few good notches as well. The one whose groping hands I'd had to avoid all evening spotted me the second I stepped back through the door.

"Hey, there's the hot serving wench," he yelled loud enough that I could hear him over the booming din of the crowd. "We need another bottle of ketchup." To prove his point, the jerk lifted the bottle and squeezed it in his meaty fist. Ketchup sprayed everywhere.

Cursing under my breath, I grabbed a new bottle of ketchup from my station. I couldn't stop myself from glancing down at the action below as I walked across the third platform where the fraternity was sitting. Quinn's helmet was on but he was standing off to the side with his horse waiting for his turn at the joust. I was relieved that his face was hidden by the helmet.

I smacked the ketchup down on the table and had to lean out of the way of the guy's grabby hand. I nearly pitched myself down the steps to the second level in my frantic effort to avoid him. One more time and I was going to call the assistant manager over to ask them to behave or leave. Unfortunately, because the diners tended to get pretty fired up with drink and competition, the management had set the bar pretty high on behavior that warranted removal from the premises. But grabbing the server was definitely on the list.

"Can we get some more root beer?" a sweet young girl asked at the table on the first level. They had the front row seats, the best in the house, as long as you didn't mind the occasional clump of arena sand getting tossed onto your turkey leg.

"Yes, of course." I collected up their empty root beer pitcher and headed across the platform to my drink station. As I passed a table that seemed to be a women's night out, I heard one of the women comment that she wished they'd sat in the red section because the knight was so hot. I had to agree with her there, smart lady.

My eyes flitted down below. Quinn's joust was about to start. He'd told me more than once that he really enjoyed his job, that he looked forward to riding and jousting. Was he leaving to work for his brother? The money would be far better, but I couldn't imagine him working in an office dressed in a suit and tie.

I filled the pitcher of root beer and carried it back to the table on the first level. I poured it in glasses and placed the pitcher on the table. From above, the thick necked creep was once again yelling for my attention. I wondered if he had any idea that there was an actual medieval show going on down below.

"Server, could you bring us another pitcher of ale? And hurry up would ya?"

The worst part of all, obnoxious customers were always extra cheap with the tip, so I was going to endure his rude behavior without any compensation at the end.

A raucous cheer went up in the red section as the announcer introduced the daring, fearless Red Knight.

I returned to my drink station and picked up a pitcher of ale. "Miss, can we get another basket of bread," a polite man asked as I passed by with the beer.

"Yes, right away." I scurried across toward the frat table. I planned to just plunk the pitcher down and hurry away but the jerk picked up his glass.

His big forehead shaded his deep set eyes as he grinned smugly. "Pour it in my glass." He leaned to the side to make a point of checking out my legs. The gesture nearly made him fall out of his chair. I was sorely disappointed that he managed to stay upright.

I took his greasy glass and poured the beer, then set it down hard in front of him. I gave him a forced smile. As I spun around to get the basket of bread for my other customer, the guy's cold, sweaty hand shot up under my dress. I shrieked and jumped away from his groping hand. My right foot slipped off the step and twisted painfully. I shrieked as I tumbled down the three steps landing sharply on both knees. My right foot throbbed with unbearable pain. I was so deep in my cloud of shock and pain, it took me a second to notice that a stunned silence was making its way around the arena. It seemed everyone in the whole damn place had seen my embarrassing fall.

The deafening silence was broken by a simultaneous gasp that whooshed through the vast dining hall like a gust of wind. I lifted my face. Several of my customers were working their way over to help me but they stopped when something in the arena caught their eye. I was behind the small retaining wall that separated level one of the dining tables from the show arena, but everyone seemed to be focused on something below.

Then a flash of red was followed by heavy black boots landing on the first level of my section. Quinn had removed his helmet. He marched toward me with such a look of concern, a sob bubbled from my lips. I sat back on the step behind me and gently brought my right foot forward. My ankle was already swelling up like a ball.

Every pair of eyes in the building was on the fallen server with the swollen ankle and the knight who had hoisted himself over the barrier to come to her rescue. It would have been wonderfully romantic if it hadn't been so darn embarrassing.

Quinn stooped in front of me, not an easy task in his armor. "Are you all right, Suzy Q?" He grazed his gloved hand over my ankle. "Shit, that doesn't look good. Just a second. I need to take care of something." He straightened. The people sitting in the nearby tables craned their necks and stared up at him in awe.

"Gosh, he's even better looking up close," I heard one customer mutter from somewhere in the haze of faces. "Bigger too," someone said.

Quinn tromped past in his big boots. I looked back over my shoulder as he reached the fraternity's table. The creep who had groped me looked close to choking on his own vomit as the Red Knight approached the table.

"Quinn, no it's all right." My voice trembled from the pain.

Quinn lowered his face and said something quietly to the guy. The jerk leaned back so far to get away from Quinn's menacing glare, he fell backward. The crowd roared with laughter.

"What's happening here?" The assistant manager was breathing hard as if he had run the entire circumference of the arena. His eyes shot to my swollen ankle. "Oh wow, Suzy, we need to get you to a doctor."

The frat boy was clumsily climbing back on his chair.

Quinn turned toward Gene. "This guy grabbed Suzy and made her fall. It's your call." His big boots carried him back down the three steps. He leaned over. I circled my arm around his shoulder and he lifted me off the steps. His armor was cold and hard but I melted against him.

The crowd was cheering and stomping and chanting, 'Red Knight' as he carried me out of the dining area. I peered up at him. "I think the Red Knight just won the hearts and minds of the entire arena."

A faint smile crossed his lips. "There is only one person's heart and mind I want to win, and I'm holding her in my arms."

"I would sigh dreamily here but my ankle hurts too much. However, you can expect one in the near future."

Someone rushed to open the employee locker room and he carried me inside. Quinn's armor creaked as he lowered me onto the bench. The ankle looked even bigger. One of the theater crew came rushing in with a bag of ice. The kid's name was Gary and his color faded when he saw my ankle.

Quinn knelt down in front of me, again a difficult task considering his costume. "Doesn't look broken. Might just be a really bad sprain." He gently placed the bag of ice over it. Gary hovered nervously next to us.

"Thanks, Gary," Quinn said, apparently deciding that's why Gary was staying around.

"Uh, Quinn, the crowd is yelling for the Red Knight. Are you coming back on the field?"

Quinn's green gaze held mine as he spoke. "Nope, the Red

Knight has to help his favorite damsel get to the emergency room. The show will have to go on without me."

Gary seemed hesitant about heading off with the news that the Red Knight was done for the evening. As his damsel in distress, I didn't mind at all.

"Now sit here and don't move," he ordered. "I'm going to head over to the dressing rooms and get out of this armor." With some effort he pushed to his feet.

"I was kind of hoping you'd stay in armor and carry me into the emergency room. I think I'd be the envy of all the other patients. They might even get me into a room quicker if they thought I was important enough to be carried in by a knight in shining armor."

"I would love to fulfill the lady's wishes but I don't think I can fit in my Porsche wearing shoulder plates. You'll have to settle for being carried in by plain old Quinn Armstrong."

I reached for his hand. "There's nothing plain or old about Quinn Armstrong. I heard you gave notice that you were leaving this place. Guess your brother finally talked you into working for Plaything."

He shook his head. "Nope. It was just too hard showing up here every day knowing you weren't going to be coming home with me. I was getting kind of used to you, to us."

"I guess I was too. I haven't been the same since I walked out. Maybe we can revisit this whole thing now. My head is clear and fuckface is entirely out of my life now. Besides, if I keep eating my mom's pancakes and cupcakes, I will not be able to wear this stupid corset belt."

He bowed. "Milady, I shall return." He turned to walk out.

"By the way, what did you say to that jerk to make him fall out of his chair?"

"A knight never reveals his secrets, but I believe I tossed in the phrase *body bag* for good measure."

Twenty

QUINN

I carried the glass of wine into the bedroom. Suzy was propped up against the pillows, once again wearing my t-shirt. Her sprained ankle, now thickly wrapped, was propped up on a pillow. I handed her the glass of wine, then stretched out next to her and turned on my side to face her.

"Have I mentioned just how fucking right you look sitting in my bed," I said as I pushed my hand under her shirt to caress her skin.

"You might have mentioned it once or twice." She smoothed her palm over the quilt. "And I am rather fond of this bed."

I propped up on my elbow and leaned over to kiss her. "I don't want to be pushy—Nah fuck it. I'm going all in on it. Why don't you pack up your cute, little duffle and move back in with me?"

She rubbed her finger around the rim of the wine glass. "Well, I don't know, my room has this really cool Green Day poster and then there's my Beanie Baby collection."

I laughed as I pushed her shirt up and kissed her stomach.

"Bring the poster and the—" I looked up at her. "Did you say Beanie Babies?"

"Oh, please don't tell me that you have never heard of Beanie Babies. We might have to call this off right now."

I pressed another kiss against her belly, then pushed the shirt up above her breasts. "Are you sure about that?" I suckled her nipple lightly and she sucked in a sharp breath.

"Well, maybe I can just teach you about them," she suggested. She took a good gulp of wine and handed it to me to put on the nightstand.

I put the glass down and turned back to her. "Let's see, where was I?" I lightly pinched a nipple. She responded by arching her back and lifting her breasts higher. I lathed my tongue around each nipple.

Suzy reached down and pulled my face up to hers. "Are you sure about this, Quinn?" she asked before kissing my mouth. "Are you sure you want me to pack up my bag so we can try this again?"

"Suzy Q, I've never been more sure of anything in my life." I pressed my mouth over hers.

More Plaything

Loved *Midnight Oil?* Check out the rest of the series.

Plaything Series:
Easy Come (Trey's story)
Sweet Spot (Chase's story)
In a Bind (Zane's story)
Role Play (Aidan's story)
Midnight Oil (Quinn's story)

Plaything Box Set (Books 1-4)

About the Author

Tess Oliver is a *New York Times* & *USA Today* bestselling author of sexy romances. She's always working on new and exciting projects. You can stay up to date, and get a free book by visiting her website and subscribing to her newsletter.

www.tessoliver.com
toliverbooks@gmail.com

Printed in Great Britain
by Amazon